Bristol Short Story Prize Anthology

Volume Six

BRIST◉L

First published in 2013 by Bristol Review of Books Ltd,
Unit 5.16 Paintworks, Bath Rd, Bristol BS4 3EH

ISBN: 978-0-9569277-4-3

A CIP catalogue record for this book is available from the British Library

Cover designed by Emily Nash
www.emilynashillustration.com

Layout designed by Dave Oakley, Arnos Design
www.arnosdesign.co.uk

Printed and bound in Great Britain by ScandinavianBook.co.uk,
Bloomsbury, WC1H 9BB

www.bristolprize.co.uk
www.brbooks.co.uk
@bristolprize

Contents

Introduction

Welcome to the sixth Bristol Short Story Prize anthology. Of course, it is the nature of these introductory messages to celebrate the continued success of the prize and the multitudinous merits of the stories but I think it is a fair assertion to say that this volume is the most impressive collection to date.

Each panel has the opportunity to judge the prize for two consecutive years and for Anna Britten, Bidisha, Christopher Wakling and I this was our second chance to reconvene and grapple with a longlist of tremendously good stories. The stories were all read anonymously, the writers' identities hidden until the proofs were prepared for publication. So, the stories had to speak for themselves, there were no introductions, no preconceptions, just the title and first line to draw the reader in. It was one of the most enjoyable aspects of the judging process; each story was a fresh encounter, a new window opening. It meant of course that there were huge demands on those first few lines to stand out amongst so many strong submissions; the writing had to lure us in and compel us to suspend all life beyond the few stapled pages in our hands.

Of the forty stories on the longlist each of us was required to select twenty and to nominate our top three prior to our final judging meeting. It was an incredibly hard task, testament to the richly accomplished longlisted stories. As we met to decide upon the shortlist we knew there would be strong favourites and dislikes, of course, but it was far more impassioned than that, we each had stories we would advocate. The gloves were off. As Bidisha says; 'we fought for the stories that spoke to us, the ones whose language we admired, whose humour we responded to and whose ideas made us think. But we also conceded places where other judges' taste clashed with our own'.

There is no easy way to define what we were looking for when deciding upon the shortlist, but as Bidisha suggests the best way to describe it is that we went for stories which 'spoke to us'. For Anna there was a quality which she responded to, in particular: 'I enjoyed anything that demonstrated bravery - in its premise, language, choice of characters - and am really pleased with how many original voices we have in the anthology'. In this anthology you'll find your disbelief suspended by a mysterious arrowhead on a battlefield, a boy who can stop time and a trans-dimensional time portal. You'll hear the intense voice of a misunderstood pop star venting all on his blog, a cynical patient in a psychiatric ward and a father trying to reconnect with his son. You'll also find characters that are incredibly well drawn; the 'private electricity' between two people in a lab will compel one of them to share the truth about his eleventh finger.

Our winning story, *The House on St John's Avenue,* received a rapturous response during our discussion, as Anna puts it: 'I fell in love with this story instantly and wanted to shout from the rooftops about it. It manages to be hilarious, weighty, sad and surreal without once losing focus or voice. I felt very, very comfortable with this writer's abilities. It handled its easy-to-mock characters with such tenderness and truthfulness'. Christopher added that he admired its 'internal coherence' and noted that 'despite its audacity, it is funny and profound with a light touch about serious issues which you only realise at the end. I fell into it and stopped being conscious of it as I read, it is utterly convincing'.

The Breakdown is our second choice, a story of such impressive scope and such clever construction. It tells the story of Medha whose son has been killed by a leopard and as the story charts her grief it explores the profound inequalities of wealth, gender and class which contextualise Medha's life. Bidisha adds that, '*The Breakdown* is a stunning work of international, universal fiction which has the urgency, scope and depth of a novel'.

We chose *Why I Waited* as our third choice, a story narrated by Penelope about her marriage to Odysseus written with such depth and aplomb. A self-aware Penelope looks back on her marriage, thinking through all those years when Odysseus was sailing against Troy, and in the final analysis finds truth and honesty as she asks, 'do you regret it? Any of it?' Reinterpretations of Greek myths have been celebrated widely in recent years yet we felt that this story brought a freshly subversive angle in Penelope's portrayal as a fearless and empowered counter to Odysseus's mythical status.

We were transfixed by all of the stories on the shortlist, in each of them we found elements to applaud and to admire. We were truly impressed with how well conceived, constructed and executed the stories were and know that they reflect writers who, we are certain, will be worth watching. The Bristol Short Story prize is uniquely poised to deliver this high calibre of short story fiction; the prize has a grassroots power in its ability to find and showcase emerging writers, yet it is also run with great professionalism a fact which has enabled it to rise to such a prestigious international level. As writers continue to struggle amidst the clamour of the commercially-focussed publishing industry the Bristol Short Story Prize continues to distinguish itself by being a true advocate of the writer.

The Bristol Short Story Prize, also, enables students from the University of the West of England Illustration degree course to experience an aspect of the publishing industry through the annual anthology cover design project. Final year students submit ideas from which the anthology cover is chosen. Emily Nash's wonderful design is a very worthy winner, continuing the tradition of eyecatching, very distinct Bristol Short Story Prize covers. I would like to thank Emily and the other students who produced such a stunning collection of designs. Thanks also to course leaders Chris Hill and Jonathan Ward whose enthusiasm and support for the project make it such a brilliant venture.

Judging this prestigious prize reconfirmed for me the joy of short stories, their ability to encompass such depth and convey such energy in so few words. They demanded my attention and I was rewarded constantly for my engagement in the fictional worlds they took me to. Bidisha speaks for all of us in saying that judging the prize had 'taught her something wonderful: that we live in a cultural society broad enough to accommodate many voices and ways of telling'. Christopher, too, comments that judging the prize has made him more zealous about the short form and brought his literary head to bear upon what makes a good short story, he felt inspired to write more. It is this power to inspire and to create such connections between writers and readers that is the substance of great short stories.

And, with that in mind, I would like to finish off by saying a huge thank you to all the writers who submitted their stories. You have given us such enjoyment, conjured up so many remarkable ideas, sparked off countless thought-provoking discussions and truly made that unique, unsurpassable connection between writer and reader.

Ali Reynolds,
Bristol, 2013

1st Prize
Paul McMichael

Paul lives in London with Marc, his partner of 26 years. His story, *After The Rhododendrons*, was recently broadcast on RTE radio. Another is soon to be published in Chapter One Promotions's new anthology of romantic stories. He has been shortlisted in other competitions including the 2013 Fish Short Story competition.

Although he was born along the rugged coast of Ireland's north-eastern tip, he is inspired by the thought that the big city and the sublime seaside town can be as bleak or as mysterious as the other.

He has attended Creative Writing courses over the last three years in London.

The House On St. John's Avenue

(A short tale about love, family and theoretical cosmology)

I.

Eric and Jack have a dinner invite. Robert and Felipe have remodelled. There is mention of plantains. Something is bugging Robert.

We drive up and down three or four times, bickering about who should have gotten the full address from Robert. "I thought you had the number," says Jack.

"You're maps and directions," I say.

"You're the keeper of the diary," Jack says. I scan to the left. "It's got to be that one." Georgian, steps to the side up to the raised ground floor, black panelled front door. Grand sash windows, two eyes on a lop-sided grin.

"Look at the fronds on that palm," Jack says.

"That'll be Felipe." I put a hand to Jack's arm. "Can you imagine the fuss at the garden centre?"

Jack puts on his not-very-Costa Rican accent. "Is very nice. But I need more big. Like Amazon."

Some kind of jungle envy thing.

We joke about how we'll force our jaws to the floor for the whole of the obligatory tour, exclaiming 'fabulous'. We do a five-point turn in the road and park. In the porch, tea lights in blown glass holders. We ring the bell. No one answers so we ring again. A pause before Felipe answers. Robert appears behind, looking sheepish. Then it's smiles, kiss, kiss, drinks, olives, nibbles, drinks. The wine is a Puligny-Montrachet 1997. "Monstruoso," Felipe says. It clings to the side like it wants to get out and join us for dinner.

Robert pours, the wine washing into each large balloon glass and sinking into a slow, buttery vortex. We bend our snouts to the trough.

Robert is tense. I try to get him on his own to find out more or to lend an ear. "Do you need a hand with dinner ?" I say.

"No, no, all under control," he says.

We bought them a shiny digital kitchen timer from Divertimenti. We might as well have flown by in an airship with the slogan, 'It's not about cooking, it's about timing'. The hosts fuss around in the kitchen.

I say, "Jack. Guess. Contemporary modern or Costa Rican fusion." Jack is trying to tune in to the sounds from inside. I go on. "I mean, access to half the world's flora and fauna in the rainforest, and yet a diet of plantains. Just, why?"

Jack laughs a little. He lays down a blanket of shhhs and pats it into place with his hand.

"I don't trust a fruit that versatile," I say. Jack laughs again.

Rumbling from the kitchen, terse voices. We slink down into the comfy sofa and hug our drinks.

We've known Felipe for about twelve years, since he first qualified at St Barts. He was on-off with Alex at the time. It was Felipe's first big relationship.

I called him Callous Alex. Alex kept the Rolex.

Then there was Nate, the theatre nurse at the Clinic. Not the first coupling forged over medical grade steel but it ended badly. It turns out there were other eyes trained on Nate. Felipe got drunk and passed out on our couch. There were a few others, fleeting. Then one weekend in Brighton he met Robert. It seemed unlikely. A plastic surgeon. A barman.

"Six months," said Jack, "seven if he's lucky."

"The first sunny day." I said.

But Robert moved quickly and firmly from one domain of being in the world to quite another and now it's been seven years and Jack and I are absolutely and completely chuffed for both of them.

Felipe is at the door with Robert.

"We do tour of the house," he says.

All very formal. That our approval should mean something feels good.

"Lovely. Dying to see what you've done," says Jack. Robert goes to top up the wine. Jack raises a hand to his glass. "Driving."

The tour starts. Their new place is lovely, a restrained period restoration. Jack and I are a bit jealous: downstairs, all light and grace; bathroom, serenity floor to ceiling; storage space, walk-through to master bedroom (the bastards).

Felipe shuffles on the stairs. Up or down? Is there more or is it back to the dining room? I see Robert thrum the fingers of both hands against the legs of his jeans.

"What's in here?" says Jack from the rear of the party. A closed door on the other side of the master bedroom.

Felipe steals a glance at Robert. "Oh…is nada," he says, his eyes flickering to Robert.

I knew it. What's in that room. I'm dying.

"Let's show them," says Robert.

Felipe hesitates then thunders back up to the landing. He jiggles

Roberts's arm. "Not now. Is not so good, come down, let's have dinner, yes?" Robert is unmoved.

II.

Secrets unveiled. A startling moment involving a cuddly toy.
Eric takes up novelty swearing.

Robert wrings his hands for a moment. "We said we would tell them," he says to Felipe. "I can't keep it a secret any longer." He approaches the door.

I feel like a nervous Alice before the rabbit hole. The door cracks, pastel blue walls inside. Another few inches. "A nursery!" I clamp a hand to my mouth. I look at Robert then back to the room. "Oh. My. God, you're pregnant! A baby. Wow, guys, a baby. Jack, we'll be uncles."

Jack says, "That's wonderful, Felipe, Robert, fantastic."

The room is almost ready, a step-ladder rests against a tall unit in the corner. I'm happy for them. "When is it, when is the big day?" I look at the two of them. Smiles of a kind, but not the unruly grins that say 'we're going to be dads'. There must be something else. Maybe there was a miscarriage. That would be terrible news. Then it comes to me. "Twins, no way. You're having twins!" I start a little up and down dance. I go to Felipe. "Is it yours?" I swivel. "Robert's?" I float off-piste on the wine. "No, no, I know, one of each!"

"Eric" says Jack.

Jack can say no with his eyebrows so I'm silenced.

"Not twins," says Felipe, "but sí, we are going to have a baby."

Then why so serious?

Robert goes on. "We didn't want to say before…."

Jack says, "So...how...where."

"America," says Robert. "Surrogacy."

"Is everything okay? So far?" Thoughtful Jack. One step ahead of me.

They might not have wombs but they'll be worried and the poor woman is thousands of miles away.

"Muy bien," says Felipe, "with the baby, todo muy bien."

"Whose...you know...which of you...," says Jack.

He means who jizzed. Everyone's first question. It stands to reason. There is an egg and there is a sperm and that makes the donors the mum and the dad. The biological ones. Except they're not *Mum* and *Dad*, though it's mostly *Mum* in parenthood, isn't it? It was with mine, bless her grey hairs.

So here we have an egg, a borrowed womb. Mums? Dad and Dad? I raise my glass to the bold purpose of it all.

Felipe speaks. "We wait to find Latino egg donor. Rosa. She is from Arizona but la familia is Costa Rica."

So now we know the *how* and the *where*, but who jizzed? I think, that must be the reason for the tension between them now. Maybe since the baby is doing well, Robert regrets letting Felipe be the father. Maybe he dreads the first time they will go Costa Rica and have the arms of Mamá Figueres clutch her grandchild and whisper in Spanish about how her little man is going to grow up big and strong like his grandfather and 'is he on solids yet' and 'does he like plantains' and 'tell your *special friend* he can sleep in the spare room'.

Maybe I'm reading too much into this.

Felipe moves, looks askance at Robert. "There is some… thing." He searches Robert's face. There's high price to that look.

"Something?" Jack says.

"Not something. A thing," says Robert.

"A thing?" I say.

"It's an opportunity too, Felipe," says Robert.

My mind is a swirl. A giant baby? Disasters medical, legal, financial present themselves.

"You need to see it really," says Robert. He turns to Felipe. "I'll go down to the kitchen. What are you going to use?"

Felipe looks around, picks a grey and white rabbit from the chest of drawers. "Softie" he says.

Robert bounds to the door, leaps the stairs. He shouts up, "Ready!" He's in the kitchen I think, just below us.

Felipe takes the stepladder and places it near the corner of the room. He looks up then nudges the back feet an inch or two here and there. He goes to the brushed chrome panel by the door and touches one of the controls. Light floods the room. He mounts the steps and stretches out an arm. "Just watch," he says. For a moment he holds the toy by the feet, its toothy smile inverted to a rictus grin. He lets go.

The evening splits, a before and an after. I hear myself sniggering during the rabbit's fall toward the deep-pile crush of the carefully considered mid-blue carpet. I imagine Jack's verbal dismay at the build-up to the cheap laugh at our expense. But, as the rain slants inwards to lash the window panes, and with a quickening March wind asking to be let in to the warmth at the house on St. John's Avenue, the rabbit disappears.

Just disappears. Mid-fall. Gone.

"Fuck," says Jack.

Understated.

In words passed through the vortex of shock and mediated by the leviathan Puligny-Montrachet 1997, I clasp a hand to my forehead. "Holy Fuckness, Felipe. Holy Mother Fuckness."

III.
Robert pulls a rabbit out of the extra-dimensional space-time discontinuity. He is eager to explore, Felipe less so. Jack is sober, Eric less so. There is mention of plantains.

Robert appears at the door. He's holding Flopsy Wopsy. "Tah dah! We found the wormhole after the renovations," he says. "It goes through to the kitchen."

Felipe sits on the ladder's last step rubbing his head as if the whole thing hurts.

"A wormhole?" I say.

Robert goes on. "It's like a virtual fireman's pole. But in another dimension."

"I want one," I say, "Jack, get me one."

"Eric, we live on the ground floor."

"Robert, he never gets me anything," I say. "Did I tell you he got himself new clubs? Said he would go to the golf range and it would be good for his back. Hasn't been once since then. A fickle man." I raise my glass in Jack's direction.

"Who's been with the same guy for thirteen years," says Jack.

He's right. It's sweet. I'm now a little drunk.

"Those clubs are on eBay tomorrow," I say to Robert.

Robert tries to re-impose himself. "Listen, guys, listen. It could be the most important scientific discovery since... all the other discoveries humans have ever made put together!"

"We need one of those all-night theoretical cosmologists," I say.

Jack peers up at the point in mid-air where Flopsy vanished. "So how does this work then, Robert?"

Ergo, Robert is just a barman who doesn't know what he's talking about. I make a mental note: teach Jack about the line of grace between smart and supercilious.

Robert looks like he has a ping-pong ball in his mouth, huffing and puffing to pop it out as they do on those record breaker shows. He glances at Felipe from the tail of his eye. "There's something else we didn't tell you either."

Felipe steps off the ladder. "Robert ."

"We may as well tell them that too." Robert is on a roll. "Give me your phone Eric. I won't break it or anything, promise."

I place my shiny black slab of joy into his palm. "Better not."

"Right, I'll go down and catch it. You'll need to come with me to prove this Eric. Jack, when I shout, drop it through." He turns to Felipe, who is scowling from the ladder. "Oh, Felipe, please, don't be all sulky. It's going to be great. This is amazing. We're going to be rich."

Give or take an apartment in the south of France, they are plastic surgeon rich. Felipe keeps telling me he'll do any bits of me I'm not happy with. No thanks, my bits are fine. He also tells Jack he'll do any bits of me that Jack's not happy with. I let it go.

Robert and I head downstairs. He fetches the laundry basket from the utility room.

"Ready!"

I try to focus on mid-air but my eyes swim. I miss the phone re-appearing. It thwumps from nowhere to the bottom of the wicker container. I fish it out from amongst the thick towels and tailored shirts. The front screen slides opens. It seems okay.

"Look at the date," says Robert.

I scroll. I look at Robert and smile. The date is last week. A short cut to the kitchen, and a time machine.

"Have I lost anything?" I scroll through. "Shit. Emails. I want a share of the profits for that. Ten per cent should cover it."

"Sorry," says Robert. "I forgot. Got a bit carried away."

"Robert." Felipe is at the door. "Let's discuss it, yes?" he says.

IV.
A delightful dinner. A discussion about the breach in the fabric of the universe. Plantains are consumed. Robert and Felipe argue. Eric and Jack are ringside.

Jack and I are hustled to the dining room. The papered walls and moulded ceiling puddle with the honeyed glow of big church candles. The silverware and glasses on the table are lined up like a parade of soldiers. A salad of figs and young Pecorino cheese, then leg of lamb, a kind of tagine, but with plantains (I knew it). Robert carries in a large dish, more of a small sailing vessel, brimming with impossibly green broccoli florets and French beans. "Sesame and truffle dressing," he says. Strictly no carbs but stuff yourself with everything else.

We do.

We push ourselves back from the table and stretch out.

Robert brings in a bottle of chilled Limoncello and three small glasses on a lacquered tray. I pour then lick the underside of my glass.

"Enough," says Jack.

"Me too," I say.

Robert talks excitedly about the space-time breach, its time travel possibilities. He's blethering on about human-kind's great scientific adventure at a new frontier. "It's safe for humans," he says. "I tried it first with a plantain. It *un-ripened*."

"I grew up on this fruit," Felipe says, "but I don't put my life in its hands."

I find that he does but I let it pass.

Robert places two hands in front of him. He thunders down the table. "And then I passed my saliva through the portal and sent it off for analysis." He looks around. "No change to my DNA. It still came out Anglo-Saxon. And possibly a little bit of Ghenghis Khan."

"That comes up a lot apparently," I say. Jack elbows me in the ribs.

"Very resourceful Robert," says Felipe, "but this proves nothing in medical terms. Gene mutation, epigenetics? You want to take such risks? With our baby coming?" He looks around at us. "Jack?"

"Robert, I think you're being naive," says Jack. "This isn't just about getting in the high-rolling risk takers looking for a cheap thrill. You'll have the council asking if we have a licence. The boffins will wrap the place in tin foil. The neighbours will resent you having a breach in the fabric of the universe in your house where they don't. There'll be soldiers in the front garden."

I sit up. "Soldiers?"

"In your dreams" says Jack. He eases the glass from my hands.

Felipe speaks again. "There will be a thousand cameras. Social services taking away the baby"

I bite my lips. Robert's face darkens, a low-pressure weather front moves north from the line of his lips.

"It's not just the money, Jack. And it's not just about celebrity, Felipe. Think what this could to do." He waits for a reply. "The terminally ill. We can help people. Maybe even cure them." He looks at Felipe. "Isn't that worth trying? We can do a good thing, it doesn't have to be just 'elective' time travel for the rich."

"I know such things as difference from elective to emergency," says Felipe.

True. A plastic surgeon makes his money in knowing just that. In the pause, I have time to look around the table. The ease and the banter have drained from the evening. The limoncello is out of reach and warming fast.

V.
Robert and Felipe take the argument for a tour of the house.
A time for honesty. Eric and Jack are transfixed.
Things end. Other things begin.

Felipe stands. "Robert, this is not about saving the world, is it? I remember you called me at the clinic. Remember? 'The egg has taken' you said, 'baby is growing'. But I see it in your eyes, you are less happy each day than the last."

No answer from Robert.

Felipe puts his shoulder to the point. "Is it my fault which embryos were stronger? 'More viable'. We agreed to it."

Robert squirms. He doesn't speak but there's a war inside him.

Jack rises from the chair. He says, "Er, we need to get up early so...." I rise too.

"Please, don't go," says Felipe. "You should stay. Drink." He waves us back into our seats.

I reach for the limoncello but Jack moves the bottle another inch beyond the tips of my fingers. He's mean.

Felipe turns to Robert. "Robbie. I'm telling you, forget this stupid... wormhole? It is trouble. I see nothing but blue flashing lights."

"This isn't all about me. How is it that these Central Americans can be so macho sometimes and yet they're all big Mamá's boys at heart? You want to show *Mamacita* that even if you are the gay son who ran away to London, you can still father a child. Mamá will be so pleased, won't she? 'Come home to your real family. Let Mamá help you bring up your little Inca warrior'."

Robert starts stacking plates. Cutlery goes flying. I worry about the china. The two of them move to the kitchen sniping about Mamá and embryos with varying degrees of recrimination. Jack and I turn to the other door. Robert and Felipe go past and up the stairs.

I turn to Jack. He says, "Eric, we should go home."

"I know." I put on my sympathetic face. "But I'm not leaving before the end of the show."

It's not a play in one act. After an age, an epoch, I go the door and cock my ears to the drowned cadence of the voices upstairs.

Jack comes over. We take a tiny step into the hall, daring to gaze up, as if the sound will float down like leaves to catch on our upturned faces. Robert and Felipe are on the landing again. I mouth *nursery* to Jack. He screws up his face. I mime cradling. He puts a finger to my lips and nods. I take hold of Jack's hand.

The sniping has stopped. Their tone is softer now, cotton in the place of stone. Felipe is talking. "Yes I admit it, I do want to take baby to show Mamá. Soon. You know she won't come to London to this house. But I need you to be there. She needs to see we are a family now, that you are not just my *friend*. We are not going anywhere. I'm going to be so proud of you and the baby. I could not go without you."

"I guess I didn't say what I really felt. You talked so much about going back and Mamá and then it was your sperm that fertilised Rosa's Latino egg and… I just felt myself shut out of everything, that you didn't really need me."

"Robbie. Look around you. See? My life is all about us. This, we bought in Amsterdam, you loved it so much this painting. Those big white stones in the bathroom, I picked them from the beach where we met for our first anniversary. You said I am mad. And this, we argue so much about damn light switches in the shop you wouldn't let me in the car and it's raining and then we are laughing and I am so crazy to kill you. All these things we have, Robbie, they are pinning me down, in the heart, here."

In the hall, Jack and I try to live without oxygen for a moment.

"Our children, they should have all this in their hearts too. But this space-time… elevator thing, it will take all away, destroy our world. Their home too."

"Their home?" says Robert.

"Why not? We have frozen eggs, you have sperm, we will make another little one if Rosa will help us, half Costa Rican and half English… and a little bit Ghenghis Khan. And they will need two of us Robbie, it will not be so easy for our family sometimes."

Jack and I make faces. We do a silent victory jig and threaten to push each other over onto the restored and highly polished wooden floor and reveal ourselves. I don't know why. Jack is sober. We stop and listen again. A low growl, a kind of whimper above us. I know that sound, the animal note a man makes when he buries his face in the soft curve of another's neck. I know that sound.

Jack and I scamper back to the dining room when Robert and Felipe stir upstairs. We clatter into our seats and carry on the second half of a conversation that never started. The two of them come in, apologising. Felipe fetches in a bottle of whisky, says it's a special moment. They tell us they will try for Robert's baby with the surrogate, lovely Rosa from Arizona.

"What about your hole?" I say. They stare at me.

I point up. "The breach in the fabric of the universe?"

"Well, no invites to the world's press tonight," says Robert. He looks at his husband. He takes Felipe's hand. "I was wrong. It's all about the baby now. So… we'll lower the ceiling or have it built in. Maybe more cupboards," he says.

Felipe comes round to the end of the table where he can wave a finger at both of us. "You two are the only ones who know and you must forget that you do. For our family." We raise our glasses and swear to the contract. I try not to blurt out 'what'll you do with even more storage space'. We help them clear the table. We do the long goodbyes milling around in the kitchen. "I'm just going to use the loo. Bursting," I say.

I stumble upstairs and pee for hours in the main bathroom. I wash my hands and then I stop on the landing. The door of the nursery is ajar. In my mind I see Robert rushing in to the cry of a young child in the dark hours, with the world's only trans-dimensional time portal concealed above him until the next residents of this beautiful house remodel. The chance to explore the phenomenon, this cosmological enigma, will be lost, tucked away with the tide of childhood paraphernalia that will wash ever higher in the baby and the toddler years to come. The wind and the rain outside the house on St. John's Avenue have dropped. I move unsteadily but silently across the landing. I reach for the handle.

2nd Prize
Deepa Anappara

Deepa Anappara is from India and has been living in the UK for the past five years. She is a graduate of the City University's Certificate in Novel Writing (currently known as Novel Studio) course. Her stories have won third prize in the Asham Award and first prize in the Asian Writer Short Story competition. In her previous life as a full-time journalist in India, she wrote articles on education, environment and religious violence, and her reports won the Developing Asia Journalism Awards, instituted by the Tokyo-based Asian Development Bank Institute, and the NGO Internews' Every Human has Rights Media Awards.

THE BREAKDOWN

Anger (i)

The morning something snaps inside Medha, she ignores the guards outside Locarno Estate and pushes open the front gate from which hangs a signboard: 'NO ENTRY for servants'. For five years she has obeyed this sign, not said a word about how it disgusts her, and taken the track cut through the grass to the bungalows where the floors are paved with marble and the bathroom faucets are finished with gold. Today she's spoiling for a fight. If Sonaali Didi wants to fire her, let her. A CCTV camera glowers down at her from the top of a lamp post.

'What are you doing?' a guard shouts as she hurries down the main road. Fortunately he's either too lazy or too bored to chase her.

Medha can hear Bunty's screams well before she reaches Sonaali's bungalow. *Won't go to school. I won't. I won't. Can't make me. You can't. You can't.* She's about to knock on the door when Sonaali opens it and drags Bunty out. The door slams shut behind them. The water-bottle hanging around Bunty's neck thuds against his tiny chest as he kicks and bites. *Won't won't won't. Mama bad bad bad.* Bunty's temper can make grown-ups tremble. In the evenings, when they're back in their shanties, other maids who work in the estate tell Medha that even the most generous of Diwali bakshishs can't convince them to spend a day with Monster Baba.

'You're late,' Sonaali says. Her red lipstick's smeared across her cheeks and a few strands of her shiny hair have freed themselves from her ponytail.

'Hello Bunty Baba,' Medha says and bends down to straighten his blue tie. He scowls at her but stops fighting, long enough for Sonaali to bundle him into the backseat of her car. Every day she drops Bunty to his school next to the estate before heading off to the IT company in SEEPZ where she works.

After the two leave, Medha opens the door using the duplicate key with which Sonaali has trusted her. The house is quiet. Akash, Sonaali's husband, must have already left for his office, though Medha doesn't consider what he does – writing scripts for television serials – work. She starts tidying the bedrooms, where the wardrobe doors are lying half-open. Sonaali likes to try on a couple of trousers or dresses before deciding what to wear that day, and always leaves clothes strewn across the bed and the floor.

Medha folds and sorts the clothes, and is about to close the wardrobe door when she notices something sparkly in a white cloth bag. It's a tomato-red designer sari embellished with stones and pearls, which Sonaali wears only on special occasions. She pulls the sari out, plucks out a single white pearl, and drops it into the mothball-smelling, dark depths of the wardrobe. Then she folds the sari neatly, places it back in the bag and closes the door. Hums a tune as she moves from room to room, dusting sculptures, mopping floors and washing plates. Does all her usual chores and then some more. She steals a stainless steel spoon, breaks an earthen pot in which Sonaali grows something called basil, and stamps on the plant until she's satisfied that its fat, fragrant leaves are brown and dead. With a broom and a dustpan, she sweeps up the pot's remnants and hides them under the vegetable peels in the trash can.

Numbness

That afternoon, Medha picks up Bunty from his school, outside which are two enormous, rectangular signs: 'Drive Slowly' (illustrated with a tortoise) and 'BEWARE! Leopard territory' (illustrated with a leopard lying draped over a branch). One such leopard mauled and killed her youngest son Nikhil six months ago, after which it hasn't been seen, either near the shanties or around Locarno Estate. Six months is apparently long enough for people to stop feeling terrified, and for her to stop mourning. Her neighbours no longer go in groups to fill aluminium pots with water from the main hand-pump. They comment on how gaunt Medha looks and joke about force-feeding her ladles of ghee. She pretends she hasn't heard them. She isn't sick or thin. She feels fine.

Outside the school gate, the ayahs, the smartly-dressed mothers and the children laugh, chat about tests and teachers, point at this girl's new bag or a hole in that boy's socks. It's a sunny afternoon but not hot because so close to the forest there's always a cool breeze, lakes to calm worn nerves. Holding her hand, Bunty skips all the way back to the estate. He has astonishing levels of energy for a child so plump. She sees a smooth white pebble by the road, picks it up and ties it to the edge of her sari's pallu, so that the stone's weight will keep tugging at her shoulder. At the front gate, which she's allowed to access when she brings Bunty home, the guards berate her for breaking the estate rules that morning.

'Grrrrrrr,' Bunty growls. 'Oye, tu log just shut up.' His outburst silences the guards.

At the bungalow, she bathes Bunty, feeds him lunch, and starts cooking snacks and dinner for the family. He plays with his many toys and tablets on the kitchen floor. Once or twice, he sends a helicopter her way and laughs, pressing the remote against his stomach, as she pretends to be frightened.

For reasons she hasn't figured out as yet, Bunty saves his worst tantrums for others. Once she heard Sonaali tell the neighbours, an elderly couple who have come back to Mumbai after a long stint in America, 'Medha's very good with him. She takes better care of him than of her own children.' This is probably true. She doesn't see much of Mayank, her eldest who's twelve and growing taller by the second, or Shashank, who's ten and too argumentative for his own good. She launders their clothes, scrapes together money for their football classes, and scolds them if they stay out late to play, but she does it out of habit, the way she imagines she can dive into a pond and drift, weightless as a leaf, or sink, her eyes open under the surface of the green-tinted water.

Denial

For a moment when she wakes up the next morning, she forgets all that has happened. She has dreamt of Nikhil and, in her dream, they walked on a beach as a golden sun slipped into the sea. This is only in part a dream. A month before he died, Sonaali, Bunty and Akash had gone to England on a holiday, and Medha had celebrated her time off by taking the children to South Mumbai (her husband had stayed back to sleep or drink). They had climbed the hundred-and-eight steps to Babul Nath temple, admired the animal-shaped hedges around the Hanging Gardens, and ridden a ferris wheel on Chowpatty Beach. Nikhil had collected pebbles of all colours and shapes at the beach and brought them home.

Now Medha walks to the white plastic table in one corner of the shack where, next to the children's books, there are three glass jars filled with stones, some of which she brought home after Nikhil's death. She turns the jars, watches the stones catch the golden light of the morning sun streaming through the holes in the corrugated iron sheets that form the walls of their home. Her husband's lying drunk on the ground. He makes hooch illegally inside the forest, but he must drink more than he sells, because he has never brought any money home.

Her children have already washed their faces, combed their hair, and are dressed in their school uniforms. Sometimes she looks at them and the thought crosses her mind that Nikhil was brighter than the two of them put together. He was at the top of his class, and all his teachers said he would grow up to become a doctor or an IAS officer. Only now can she freely admit to herself that Nikhil had been her favourite child.

After the children leave, she opens the bag in which she stores Nikhil's clothes and books. She closes her eyes and goes back to her dream. 'Aai, shall we get some mango kulfi?' Nikhil asks her as they walk on the beach. 'It's so sweet, so nice and cold.'

Bargaining

Medha's on her way to Locarno Estate when an old man, a morning walker dressed in a white T-shirt and white shorts, comes running towards her. 'Quick, find someone, call for help, do something,' he pants. 'A leopard... it's... Baburam... eating.'

She has visited this scene in her nightmares: she stays frozen as the leopard's yellow eyes lock with hers and it crouches and jumps, its whiskers quivering, its claws reaching for her jugular. But now she behaves in a precise, considered fashion. She runs back the way she came, stops a couple of joggers from Locarno Estate she had passed earlier, and tells them about the leopard. Along with the old man, she leads the joggers up a steep, wooded trail. Birds chirp on trees and a stray dog barks, raising an alarm to warn its friends. By the time they reach it, the leopard has dragged the man off the trail. Medha sees a line of blood, bits of flesh, and then the body itself, two legs eaten up to the bone. A jogger screams. The old man shakes his head. 'They have nothing to eat in the forest anymore,' he tells her. 'You can't blame the leopard.'

The joggers fish out their mobile phones and start calling the police, the guards at the estate, their families. Medha leaves them to it and sprints towards her sons' government school. Did she have a premonition that the leopard, maybe the same one that killed Nikhil, would return? Is that why she has been behaving oddly? At the school, she warns the watchman and peeks into her younger son's classroom. The cell phone Sonaali has given her, not out of kindness but only so she can reach her whenever she wants, starts ringing.

'There's a leopard in our area. It has killed a man,' Medha tells her.

'Shit,' says Sonaali. 'I can't be late for work.'

Medha calls Shashank out of the classroom. 'The leopard's back,' she whispers. 'No matter what, don't go anywhere alone. Gather all the kids from our area and walk home together, okay?' He looks embarrassed about her turning up outside his classroom but he nods. He knows this is serious.

Outside the school, she tells herself that the leopard will not be hungry for another couple of days. By then, the forest department would have laid traps to catch it. Baburam, the dead man, was an advocate who lived in the estate and not in the shanties, so the police and the forest department won't ignore his death the way they ignored her son. Just in case, she prays. *I will be good, I promise, God. From now on, I will take good care of Sonaali Didi's plants. I won't tear her clothes. I will be a better mother to my children. I will love Mayank and Shashank as much as I loved Nikhil. I wasn't thinking straight before. Please forgive me. Please, please, please.*

Despair

Medha, sweating, exhausted, gets to the bungalow and finds Sonaali hasn't yet left for her office.

'Make sure Bunty doesn't wander anywhere when you pick him up from school,' she says. 'Come back with all the other maids, you hear me?'

Bunty's school has a tall, spiked iron fence around it, and is only a few feet from the estate, whereas her children have to trudge a couple of kilometres to and from their government school, separated from the forest by a mossy, broken boundary wall.

'We will be careful, hai na Bunty?' Medha says, looking at the child, who's sitting on a white sofa, scrunching his nose.

Sonaali hangs around the house, calling up her colleagues and apologising for being late, having long, repetitive conversations with Akash on the phone about whether it's safe to send Bunty to school or not. Bunty makes the decision for them by stomping his feet and screaming TAKE ME TO SCHOOL RIGHT NOW I SAY. He has an arts project he wants to show off to his classmates. 'This boy,' Sonaali says and picks up her laptop bag and car keys. 'I will come back home early today.'

Medha starts mopping the floor on all fours, pushing a bucket half-filled with water around the living room, dunking the wiping cloth in the water and wringing it every few feet. Sonaali's comment follows her around, tormenting her: *I will come back home early today.*

On the night Nikhil died, Sonaali had made Medha stay back because she was throwing a party and needed help. Until midnight, Medha had stood in the kitchen, her feet hurting, her eyes watering, rolling out gobi parathas and frying pappads, refilling ice buckets and peanut trays. Meanwhile, back at the shanty, Nikhil had gone outside to pee, unaccompanied by his father (who was too drunk) or his brothers (who were sleeping). This was when the leopard killed him.

Medha returned to work just a week after Nikhil's death, and thanked Sonaali for not docking her pay. The closest Sonaali came to acknowledging her loss was a couple of months ago, when she told Medha about how she had consulted a numerologist after years of failing to conceive. On his advice, she had added an extra 'a' to her name and, in a year, Bunty had been born. 'You should see him. He's very good. He will help you heal,' she had said, without mentioning the numerologist's fees, which was probably ten times the monthly salary she gave Medha.

Now she dips her hands in the bucket of water that has turned a murky grey, looks at the green veins splayed out on her wrist. One cut with Sonaali's gleaming, sharp knife, and it will be over. Even this burst of emotion, Medha knows, has come too late. Instead of lying curled up on a mat, crying, all this time she has been busy *surviving*. Last week, someone new to the neighbourhood asked her how many children she had, and first she said *three*, and then she said *no, sorry, I meant two*.

Anger (ii)

By the time Medha reaches home, both Locarno Estate and the area around the shanties look deserted. Windows and doors are bolted shut. Curtains are drawn. Neighbours don't lean over boundary walls to gossip. Children are locked up inside with their video games or books. On the wooded trail where the advocate was killed, the forest department has set up a trap with a hen tied inside. There's a second trap behind Medha's shack, which abuts the forest. Here a stray dog has been used as bait. All night the dog barks or whines plaintively and, lying next to her on a frayed mattress, her sons sleep fitfully as its cries echo through the forest. Only her useless husband finds quiet in his hooch.

The next morning, Medha hands Mayank a small package to hide in his satchel. It's a blunt kitchen knife wrapped in a newspaper, to be taken out only if he sees the leopard. 'Don't tell anyone about it,' she says, and he looks grave and proud, as if Lord Shiva himself has given him a trident for protection.

Outside the shacks, women talk about the difficulty in peeing into buckets at night. 'It's okay for men, but how long can we keep doing this? They better catch that leopard soon,' a neighbour says. Their makeshift toilets are behind the shrubs in the forest and, to frighten the leopard, they go in groups, singing loudly or beating an upside-down bucket with a stick.

The dog's alive and asleep inside its trap.

A bearded man walks around the shacks, warning everyone that the municipality's going to demolish their settlement, because it's illegal and encroaches on the forest.

'Where did you hear that?' Medha asks him.

He spits on the ground and doesn't answer her. Instead he says, 'Why don't they send their bulldozers to the estate? When the rich folk build golf courses and swimming pools, it doesn't destroy the forest or the leopards. But us living, us breathing, that's a big-big crime.'

Afterwards, Medha walks with her boys to their school, and hold their hands at the gate even as they try to wriggle free. The school watchman tells her he doesn't have to do any night-shifts until the leopard's caught. The vendors and the juice stall owners in the area have also decided to down shutters by seven in the night. 'They're going to lose a lot of money,' the watchman says and grins, as if pleased with this prospect.

At Locarno, Sonaali mutters something about the leopard showing up in the footage from a CCTV camera. The trap in the woods is lying empty, she says. The hen inside it has mysteriously disappeared. *God knows what's going on.* Sonaali rushes around the house, gulping down her black coffee, microwaving her two-minute oats, pinning a handkerchief to the front pocket of Bunty's shirt, and making him wear a lanyard around his neck with a laminated card that has his name and contact details. Bunty waves Medha goodbye by telling her what he wants to eat when he returns from school: 'Chicken Maharaja Mac', which is his favourite McDonald's burger.

Medha cleans up after them, wondering if Sonaali has noticed the missing basil pot. She cooks the fish that's stinking up the fridge and fashions cutlets out of them. Later in the afternoon, outside Bunty's school, the mothers in their jeans and the ayahs in their clean salwar-kameezes frown at her because she smells of fish and frying. Bunty sniffs the air as he hands her his bag and says, 'Maharaja Mac, give give give.'

'First we will go for a walk to the lake,' she tells him.

'Mama said not to go anywhere.'

'They have already caught the leopard. Your teachers didn't tell you?'

Bunty frowns. She bends down, loosens and reties his shoelaces. The crowd at the school thins. She holds his hand and they walk down the road, away from the estate, until Medha's sure no one can spot them.

'Chalo, let's have some fun,' she says.

They head to the wooded trail where the trap has been set. It's empty as they pass it. Bunty starts to complain. *Don't want. Don't want. Don't want. No no no no.*

'Shut up, you stupid boy,' she says with such vehemence that Bunty bites his lips, and tears fill his eyes. She drags him up the track and stops only when she spots leopard scat and pugmarks. Her cell phone starts to ring. Sonaali calls them at 1.30 pm every day to make sure they're home, and to have a chat with Bunty. Medha throws the phone into the green undergrowth. The phone trills. Crickets shriek. Bunty cries.

What now? Is she going to leave him inside the trap as a bait? Is she going to fight the leopard with her bare hands, kill it for having killed her son?

She picks up Bunty, who's heavy and snotty, and holds him tight. His small hands encircle her neck. His breath, his tears, burn her skin. She pats his back, puts him down, and they head back to the estate.

Two guards and Sonaali's elderly neighbours are standing outside the bungalow. Sonaali must have called them up to find out what was going on.

'There she is,' a guard says in an accusatory tone. 'She's been using the main road, our queen of Locarno.'

'Why didn't you come back with the others?' the America-returned woman asks.

'Why aren't you picking up your phone?' her husband asks.

'Is this the time to wander around with a child?' the guard asks.

Medha hands over Bunty and his bag to the woman. She takes out Sonaali's duplicate house key, which she keeps safe in a pouch tied to her sari, and gives it to the man.

'What's this?' he asks. 'What do you think you're doing?'

Acceptance + Guilt

When she gets back to the shack, her husband's sitting outside, smoking a beedi. He doesn't ask her why she's home at this hour of the day. In his world, the sun rises and sets when he thinks it should. Sometimes she envies the simplicity of his life, his ability to seek and find comfort in a bottle of hooch. But the restlessness inside her – no bottle can calm it, she doesn't think so.

'We're leaving,' she tells him.

'What?'

'I heard there are shacks for rent in Govandi. We will move there. There are plenty of schools nearby for Mayank and Shashank.'

'What about your job?'

'I have left it.'

'Are you mad?'

'I'm going to pick up the kids from the school and go to Govandi right now. To look around. Do you want to come?'

'You need money to move.'

'I have saved up a little bit.'

'I'm not going anywhere. My work's here. What will I do in Govandi?'

'Your work?' Medha laughs.

'Enough,' he shouts. 'Churel,' he abuses her as he walks off into the forest, where day after day leopards have failed to touch him. Perhaps they are put off by the stench of hooch.

From the plastic table inside, Medha picks up one of the glass jars packed with pebbles. She steps outside and twists its lid open, tips the jar over, and empties the pebbles onto the ground. Dust rises into the air. She wishes, once again, that she had been home to stop her son from stepping out.

What kind of mother is she?

The worst there is.

A chameleon suns itself on the trunk of a tree. The settlement is quiet. All the children are at school, and their parents are out working, hawking vegetables, driving autorickshaws, fixing tyre punctures. The dog inside the trap scratches the floor. In the forest beyond the cage, Medha thinks she can see the upward curve of a long, spotted tail, the flash of a leopard's pointed, white fangs. She straightens her back and waits, holding the empty jar close to her heart.

3rd Prize
Anne Corlett

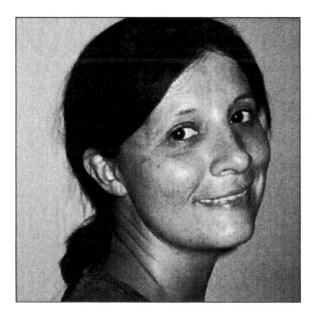

Anne Corlett is a criminal lawyer. She is still unsure how this happened, given a firm intention to work in publishing, two linguistic degrees and a stint as an etymologist. Her first novel, *Telemachus*, is currently out on submission, and she is working on her second. She has written articles for various publications, and has recently ventured into short fiction. She was a finalist for this year's *Mslexia* short story competition. She has also taken part in several short story events. She is originally from Tyneside, but now lives near Bath with her partner and two small children.

She rants regularly at http://consummatechaosblog.blogspot.co.uk/

Why I Waited

"**I** never wanted to go, my love."

He repeated those words so many times in those last days. It was as though they were a mantra against everything he had done.

And every time I gave the same reply. "I know you didn't."

I knew it wasn't quite true, but I'd come to an accommodation with the various shades of truth by then, in a way I could never have imagined all those years ago when Odysseus first brought me home to Ithaca.

It's funny how people fuss and worry over the little lies. When Telemachus was about three, he'd steal fresh-baked biscuits from the kitchen, then deny it. He'd stand there with the crumbs still on his face saying "It wasn't me," while the cook fumed and threatened and demanded that he confess.

But we'll forgive the big, world-changing lies, as long as they entertain us, as long as they're bold enough, epic enough to be recorded for posterity and called the truth.

Take the twenty year absence, for example. I'm always astonished that anyone would believe that it could really take someone ten years to get home. There's only so much ocean, after all. No matter how many sea-gods you offend, ten years is pushing it a little.

It was five years, all in. Four at Troy. Another on that farcical journey home. And if my beloved husband had spent a little less time telling tall tales of wooden horses and actually paid attention to the stars and the currents, he'd have been back in a matter of weeks.

Not that he'll ever admit it, of course. He'll look you in the eye and tell you that lotus-eaters drugged his men, or that his sailors stole his bag of magic wind.

There was only ever one wind-bag on that voyage, if you ask me.

I was a child when we were married, though I was sure, back then, that my three years of moon-bleeding made me a woman. I was in a fever to be wed. I dreamed of holding a man's heart in my hand, of ruling his hearth and home. I imagined myself waiting, proud and beautiful, on the harbourside to greet my eager, homecoming husband after a journey or a campaign. But mostly, I dreamed of the wedding, of the flowers and the dancing and the whispers about my own unsurpassed magnificence.

And then, all at once, the dancing and feasting was over, and I was on my way to Ithaca.

Young girls see no further than the altar, never realising that beyond the wedding lies a marriage and many years of belonging. The wedding is just an extension of girlhood, all dressing-up and masquerade. Wifehood begins at the marriage bed and sex is non-negotiable once you've promised to obey.

He didn't force me, or hurt me.

Not too much, anyway.

But he was due his marriage rights, and he took them, kindly but firmly.

When it was done, he lay beside me in the great bed that he had made for me, anchored, eccentrically and immovably, through the floor by an olive tree. He kissed my tears away, and span me pretty tales of the days and years to come, when I would be the living heart of his home, as patient and constant as that olive tree, his equal in all matters.

That was his first lie.

"I never wanted to go, my love."

I wondered sometimes, as I held his querulous hand in mine, if he had come to believe his own words.

I couldn't blame him if he had. They say that Helen launched a thousand ships, but Odysseus spawned a thousand stories. There was something about him that had caught the imagination of the world, and the world told him what it wanted him to be. On every page of every bard's tale he towered, colossus-like, his stature matching that of the gods he claimed to have offended. Who could blame him if he was caught and entranced?

I was on those pages too, although few writers gave page-space to a Penelope who was more than a caricature. The patient wife. The epitome of faithfulness. Sometimes I found myself almost slipping into the belief. It was a comfortable fantasy, my own face, proud and unyielding, gazing across the empty harbour day after day, waiting for my one true love to return and give me meaning once again. But it's not an illusion I can maintain for very long. There's only so much waiting you can fit into a year after all. It's just about long enough to say "Where in the name of the gods do you think you've been?" but not long enough to say "All is forgiven. Welcome home my lord and master."

Anyway, of course he wanted to go.

They all did.

Helen hadn't toed the party line. She had been granted a most high place as Menelaus's queen, in exchange for her virtue and her obedience, and then she'd broken her bargain by lifting her skirts for the first pretty boy to come her way.

They all went off like a cackle of old women, all those great lords and leaders of men. It was as though they thought that if they protested loud enough, they might forget that she'd just become the whore they'd all wanted her to be, in the privacy of their own heads and the dark of their bedchambers.

So off they went to clamour at the walls of Troy, swept along by righteous indignation, hell-bent on returning her to her proper place, and sending a message to all the other wilful women of the world, that such insubordination could not be tolerated.

Odysseus didn't paint it quite like that of course. He spun me a love-story, a lament for poor, broken-hearted Menalaeus. He painted such pictures of the topless towers and the thousand ships that, fool that I was, I found myself caught by the glamour of the story and almost forgot what a silly, fickle creature Helen was.

"Go," I told him. "You should go."

"What about the baby?" He feigned reluctance, his hand resting on my swelling stomach.

"You won't be gone long," I said. "And I'll have my women. Babies are women's work."

He nodded. Babies were women's work. Disobedient women were men's work.

And so he went. His sails bright and new and his eyes already fixed on the horizon, even as I kissed him goodbye.

But I had little time to think of what was happening beneath the walls of Troy, because I was distracted by the battle being fought within my own body, as my growing child waged war on the last remnants of my girlhood. My waist yielded and swelled to give him the room he demanded, and my once neat breasts grew unwieldy, leaking traces of the milk he would require when he deigned to arrive in the world.

I remember little of the birth. Just a vague, terrifying sense of being out of control, my body taking over and hurtling me towards some reckoning. My women had spoken of the empowerment of birth, of the triumph of bringing life, single-handed, into the world. But the faint flashes I have are of hands on my body, faces glaring and voices demanding my obedience. My baby was, by all accounts, dragged into the world, as I lay limp and exhausted, and no longer caring what became of me.

In contrast, the days that followed are clear and sharp as glass. I could not tell where I ended and the world began, but I absorbed everything. My son's blue eyes. The cool, still ocean. My baby's cry. The answering call of the gulls. I looked into the sky and I was brittle-blue. I gazed at the fire and I was flame-red. I was the opposite of colour-blind. I looked upon the world and the world told me what to be.

In time I returned to myself and, like most young mothers down the ages, I became an extension of my child. He cried and I ran to snatch him up. He pawed at me and I dropped whatever task was to hand and lifted him to my breast. He smiled and I was lost.

Troy fell.

Helen was back with her husband-king, for better or for worse. I felt an unexpected, faint regret for her, for her marriage-bed was hardly going to be a happy place, as she grew old next to a man who would never forgive her.

But another year turned full circle before my own errant husband returned.

He mis-timed his arrival into harbour and no-one was there to receive him and give him his five years of dues. Instead he slunk home, alone and unannounced. When the servants woke they found him, ostentatiously travel-stained, dozing beneath his sea-cloak before the hearth.

I have no idea why. It's not as though he didn't know where the bedchambers were.

I toyed with him a little. Pretending not to know him, that sort of thing. It was a petty, pointless past-time, since we both knew I'd take him back. Ithaca was his, after all.

I was his, after all.

"I never wanted to go."

"I know," I said, stroking his age-creased brow.

I might have believed that if he'd only left me once. But he'd been back a matter of weeks before I caught him on the harbourside, trying to talk his old shipmates into some new venture.

He wasn't even repentant. He just went off into one of his speeches. I told him I didn't care if he thought there was no profit in an idle king. There was certainly profit in a happy wife and a peaceful life and if he went he'd see how well I'd wait this time.

He seemed a little put-out. He clearly still had an image of me as that gullible girl-wife he'd left five years before.

He still went, though.

"Just a quick trip," he told me, his eyes already on the horizon.

He came back full of tales of a one-eyed giant. I didn't challenge him. Already the songs of brave Ulysses were a verse longer. I didn't have the energy to be the sour note, the sour wife in the midst of the adulation.

And so the pattern was set. He'd stay a while, swearing that out in the world, he thought of nothing but me. And then the wind would change and he'd be gone beyond the horizon again.

It was harmless enough, for the most part. An ageing sea-lord and his ageing crew, re-living old glories. A spot of gambling here, a brawl or two there, while he wore out his welcome in the palaces of our neighbours.

Once, the Phaeacian king's men brought him home and left him to sleep off his roistering on our shores.

I never did find out what happened to his ship that time.

But sometimes I'd see the warning signs, and I'd know that one of the enemies of wifehood had reared her head.

The practiced seductress, turning men into witless beasts. The young temptress, full of innocent guile. He'd be gone for a while and, when he returned, he'd have that look in his eyes that told me, better than a confession, that he'd been whispering tales in another woman's ear.

I always got it out of him in the end, although he seemed to think I truly believed that Circe was an enchantress, Calypso a scheming nymph. I never told him otherwise.

Why would I? It wasn't as though I could claim any moral high-ground. He knew, and I knew, that one or two of those 'suitors' had been given more than hospitality.

I never intended to be unfaithful. But it seemed that every time Odysseus disappeared on a tryst, some pretty boy would come to the door. And every time I'd weave my resolve, telling myself that it would be nothing more than a few words and smiles, maybe a kiss or two. But what I wove by day, I undid by night, as I lay in their arms in that immoveable marriage bed.

It was strange how determinedly everyone overlooked my infidelities. It seemed as though the further I slipped from my pedestal, the more desperately they heaved me back up, singing loudly of my unsurpassed faithfulness, as though to drown out any confession I might make.

Eventually, I realised what they were doing. There'd already been a Helen in our generation and they didn't want another. They needed me to be a foil to her, a solid reminder of the unquestioning place of womankind, a reassurance of the natural order of things.

And perhaps they needed me as a foil to Odysseus himself. A woman, steadfast before her hearth and household gods, to lend virtue to her errant husband. What other reason could there be for his place in posterity? He had brawled and cheated and sulked his way halfway round the world, screwed at least two other women – and don't even get me started on Scylla – and had generally been the antithesis of everything a hero is supposed to be.

Yet they loved him for it, penning tales that looked set to last a millennium, never uttering a word of incredulity as his rhetoric spiralled higher and higher, until every man he'd ever encountered was a god or a demon, and every woman who'd ever smiled his way was a witch or a medusa.

Through it all, there was one redeeming feature in his life.

Me.

I gave them all hope that, no matter what their failings, no matter what their faults, they too could find safe harbour and forgiveness.

They didn't love him because he was a hero.

They loved him because he wasn't a hero, and because I loved him anyway.

"I never wanted to go, my love."

His hand was limp in mine, and I could feel that his pulse, always speeding on to the next excitement, the next enticement, was finally slowing and fading.

"I know," I said. "Rest now."

His grip tightened, and he half-rose from his pillows, fixing me with an urgent gaze.

"Tell me one thing," he said. "Did you believe it? Any of it?"

I smiled and kissed him. "Not a word of it, my love."

His eyes continued to search my face and I reached out to touch his cheek with the back of my fingers.

"You tell me one thing then," I said.

"Anything." He caught my hand in his and turned his face to kiss my palm.

"Do you regret it? Any of it?"

It was my one remaining fear. After all we'd done, after all the striving, and after the hard-won peace of our later years, I was afraid that it would be for nothing more than a clutch of ragged regrets.

He looked at me for a long moment, and then his old, reckless smile flashed across his face.

"Not a moment of it, my love."

Michael Bird

Born in Bristol and now based in Bucharest, Michael Bird is a journalist specialised in South-East Europe, writing in-depth features on subjects including the abuse of illegal drugs such as Krokodil, stray dogs, the controversial new anti-ballistic U.S missile shield and exposing racist content in British press coverage of Romania and Bulgaria. Now editor for investigative journalism website theblacksea.eu, he has previously written for *The Independent on Sunday, ak13, Design Week* and the *New Statesman*. His published short fiction includes *The Happy Parents* (pulp.net), *Reindeer Salami* (Wells Festival of Literature) and *The Joy Ultimatum* (Hayward Gallery George Condo Prize, shortlisted).

England Doesn't Want You

GUS BROOKS

TROUBADOUR MADMAN
LIFE GAZER

POP UP X Click to exit

Gus Brooks
'A better class of scum'
OUT NOW
on Riposte Records
Contains the tunes 'England doesn't want you', 'Love after love' and
'Stained by eyeliner'
Buy it HERE
LINK

Previous News
[Archived]

30 September

Fans, me-haters or those just curious, thank you for reading my life! I expect mucho grande to seduce more of you to this blog thanks to the epic success of my new track. In this global climate of everyday disaster, can you believe we are actually selling a single? The kids aren't just sharing it gratis. 'England doesn't want you' is set to be the biggest climber this week. Rocketing up from number 30 to number three. Hold on tight, we're going STELLAR.

In case you can't hear me properly on the audio [muso critics do focus on how I 'mumble'], lyrics below:

CHORUS:
England doesn't want you
England never loved you
England doesn't want to
Be a part of you

VERSE:

England hate your food
England say it stinks
England do not care
What your mother thinks

(CHORUS)

VERSE:

England hate your music
Trainers, jeans and shirt
Says your face is stupid
And your hair is worse

(CHORUS)

BREAK:

England hate your brothers
England hate your lovers
Hate you when you work
Hate you when you don't
Hate you when you hope
Hate you when you vote
England hate your country
Even if you believe
That country be England
Sing

(CHORUS)

Comments

There are no comments

1 October

A big old smacker goes out to my smashing gal Sal for giving me the encouragement and support over all these years. All her patience and understanding has been crucial to my success. She said to me - 'Next week you will be number ONE' and she is never wrong! It's proof, darling, of all this pain we have shared over the years. Sal is the most beautiful girl in East London, which makes her the most beautiful girl in the world.

Comments

Buzzed2Infinifi
1/10/12 14:07 GMT
Kicking track. Ya made it, my son. We're with you since the beginning and now with you all the way, mate.

GavinThursday
1/10/12 14:20 GMT
Just bought the album TWICE!

MrWhite
1/10/12 14:45 GMT
When will you release the 2011 acoustic take of 'Cougar Hearts' live at the Electric Tank studios? I have found a bootleg copy, but the quality is sub-par and the vocal track is distorted. Is there a clean version available?

2 October
A mighty cheer to the boys for a brilliant win last night in the footie. Ace last minute victory thanks to Williams on the right. Cross was stupendous. What a header from Jones! Just heard from a friend who was at the game that the fans were chanting 'England doesn't want you' on the terraces. What a result! But naturally it was because someone f-ed up. And that award goes to... Jason Welland, who (as you know) missed the penalty [the

bar! OoooOF!]. As soon as the ball hit the woodwork, the chorus kicked off. It was pounding! My friend believes the song is so catchy it might become a fixture. A big LIKE goes out to England's FANS.

Comments

FlooringGoldmine
2/10/12 19:09 GMT
Discount Laminate Flooring
Factory prices laminate flooring at heavy discounts of $0.49 per square foot.
Save up to 67 per cent on retail and 33 per cent on wholesale!
We deliver anywhere!
www.discountflooringexcellentdeal.com

3 October
FACT OF THE DAY
Sammy Kane - who is a TOTALLY better singer-songwriter than me - said that when it comes to lyrics, all that matters is the chorus. If the chorus packs a punch, it's okay if the verses fire blanks [is that mixing a metaphor? Give us your thoughts!]

Comments

There are no comments

4 October
A big F. YOU goes to the Daily Herald. The 'newspaper' printed an article declaring that 'England doesn't want you' is RACIST. The article is a

complete slag-off. It selects lyrics without looking at my full vision for the song. Apparently by repeating "England hate" in my "enlisting" of the "third person singular" in a noun next to the "first person singular form for an accompanying verb" is an imitation of an "Afro-Caribbean argot" that shows I am "less than civil to Britain's black minority." The writer - Quentin Murphy-Edwards - says that "Brooks's defence may be that he is adopting an ironic stance, but will such a stance be respected in the council flats of Brixton and the destitute ex-industrial communities of Bradford and Sheffield?." Today, my HUMUNGOUS LOVE goes out to Brixton, Bradford and Sheffield. You're on the gig circuit next year, thanks to Quentin Murphy-Edwards.

Comments

TequilaSlamDunk
4/10/12 12:55 GMT
Muphy-Edwards does not now his arse from his eblow.

MrWhite
4/10/12 14:45 GMT
I am resending this message: When will you release the 2011 acoustic take of 'Cougar Hearts' live at the Electric Tank studios? I have found a bootleg copy, but the quality is sub-par and the vocal track is distorted. Is there a clean version available?

5 October
FACT OF THE DAY
It's ALL about the fans.

Comments

There are no comments

6 October

Bad news again. Gus Brooks is MAJORLY sad. I saw these news reports about some little kid in Cheshire, a Muslim boy called Khalid, who was beaten up after school by some other kids, who I guess were white or definitely not-Muslim. Anyway, they kicked him about while they were chanting 'England doesn't want you'. He is now in hospital. The radio, TV and pundits are now calling for the song to be banned. FOR THE RECORD, PEOPLE, the song is not a song against Muslim kids. I love kids. Ask Sal. One day, we'll have LOADS of them. Once the third album and tour are over.

Comments

SpockTease
6/10/12 18:05 GMT
England DOES want you, Kaled.

7 October

The news reports are LEGION. Now I spend all my time fighting them off! I had to go on TV on the ToughTalk show with the presenter, Edward Burnstone, to explain why I AM NOT A racist. We aren't allowed to connect to the video, I am told by some lawyer who apparently works for me. Therefore here is a transcript of what happened, courtesy of the TV station and my lovely PR person, Janis, who was up last night with me getting this down.

PRESENTER: What do you say to Khalid Mustafa who was attacked by pupils from his school while they were singing your latest hit?

ME: I want to say I am like really sad about this because I don't have anything NOTHING against little Muslim kids or kids of any race, creed or whatnot.

PRESENTER: You say 'England hate your brothers'. Do you mean black people?

ME: No, it means a brother who is like your brother, as in a family, not like a black brother as in a friend or a mate.

PRESENTER: You say 'England hate your food, England think it stinks'. Is that a reference to any specific cuisine, which may be particularly aromatic?

ME: Such as curry?

PRESENTER: Yes, is it about curry?

ME: No, it could be about the food of any nation. Even Germans and cabbage or Italians and pasta.

PRESENTER: So it's about race.

ME: Not just race, a people or a region in the country. Such as Newcastle.

PRESENTER: So one could forge a link between your words and any race? It's a one-size-fits-all song for racists?

ME: Let me tell you about my inspiration. This song is about me. About how I felt as a struggling singer-songwriter living in dire poverty. I was so poor. So massively poor. Not a poor you guys can probably understand with your big-time media careers and your suits and ties and nice hair. I felt left out of this country. I felt like England didn't want me. It's me that England doesn't want, not a Muslim kid in Chester.

PRESENTER: But you're successful now.

ME: That was then.

PRESENTER: So all along England did want you.

ME: It seems so.

PRESENTER: Yet you still sing the song.

ME: I once wrote a love song about wanting a girl but not having her. Later I got the girl, my lovely girlfriend of seven years. So should I stop singing that song?

PRESENTER: But don't you see? The song has become a racist's hymn.

ME: The problem is not the song, it's racism.

PRESENTER: Will you keep singing the song?

ME: It's my baby. I can't let it go.

Comments

VladimirPutin
7/10/12 12:00 GMT
This comment has been removed for legal reasons.

Robot_Pancake
7/10/12 12:45 GMT
This comment has been removed for legal reasons.

FlooringGoldmine
7/10/12 19:35 GMT
Discount Laminate Flooring
Factory prices laminate flooring at heavy discounts of $0.49 per square foot.
Save up to 67 per cent on retail and 33 per cent on wholesale!
We deliver anywhere!
www.discountflooringexcellentdeal.com

8 October

Are you listening, Quentin Murphy-Edwards and Edward Burnstone? 'England Doesn't Want You' is NOW topping the charts. Numero UNO. It is amazing. But there is bad news. I have just heard that the public radio are STOPPING playing it due to a large number of complaints. Plus a couple of commercial radio stations have also banned the song. This is ignorant and stupid. My PR Janis says this is censorship. She believes they don't want the people to hear me. When did England become a police state? Come on, fans, let's fight back!

Comments

Two_Ball_Screwball
8/10/12 11:07 GMT
This comment has been removed for legal reasons.

VladimirPutin
8/10/12 18:09 GMT
This comment has been removed for legal reasons.

WickedPedia
8/10/12 19:47 GMT
This comment has been removed for legal reasons.

13 October

Bloody brilliant gig last night! Great effort from the moshpit as soon as we slammed the opening chords for 'England'. I saw some faces in the audience that were not English as in a traditional-white-sort-of-way, so that SHOWS you it is not a racist song. Anyway, in reaction to all this BOLLOCKS in the media and the SAD way that some people have tried to exploit my song, I have decided that from now on ALL THE MONEY from 'England doesn't want you' will go to anti-discrimination groups.

Comments

SuffolkAngel
13/10/12 14:34 GMT
I think it is ace that you are raising the issue of racism in our country. It is still a huge problem and we really need to talk about it. Your song makes people talk and that is a good thing.

RollWithIt
13/10/12 14:56 GMT
THANK YOU TO YOUR SONG FOR STANDING UP FOR ALL THE REAL ENGLISH IN THIS COUNTRY AND AGAINST THESE FREELOADING IMMIGRANTS FROM ROMANIA, BULGARIA, INDIA, PAKISTAN, IRAK, AFRICA ETC...

SpockTease
13/10/12 15:20 GMT
Hey RollWithIt, I don;t think you get the song at all, mate. It is not in suport of racism it is against racism and the fact that racism is SHIT.

IranSucks
13/10/12 15:45 GMT
SpockTease - Just you wait! Soon those Ayatollas in Parliment force our kids to read the Koran in primry school.

VladimirPutin

13/10/12 16:34 GMT

This comment has been removed for legal reasons.

The_Horse_Whisperer

13/10/12 17:00 GMT

This comment has been removed for legal reasons.

HumbertX2

13/10/12 17:23 GMT

We must leave the Commonwealth, the European Union and the UN. We must be a truly independent nation. We must stop the immigrants flooding into our country. We must stop declaring our imperial heritage was bad for the world. We gave the world greatness. We gave the world the gift of England. But the world did not want it. The world did not want England. Now the only way is out.

SpockTease

13/10/12 18:06 GMT

Colonism was a riot, yeah, **HumbertX2**? What about all those massacres in Burma and India and Nigeria and other places where we killed lots of people cos they didn't like us? We have BLOOD on our HANSD.

SpockTease

13/10/12 18:07 GMT

HANDS

14 October

Gus Brooks is AMAZINGLY surprised to hear that the National Anti-Nazi Org has said it will NOT take the royalties from my song. It said it was pressured by its members to refuse. One of the guys from the org said it was like taking money from the Ku Kux Klan. I AM NOT THE KLAN, PEOPLE. Plus a couple of black, Jewish and Muslim groups have also said no to the donations. My PR Janis is FLABBERgasted. Guys. I want to help. 'England doesn't want you' wants to help. We are not racist, comprende?

Comments

TheseArentTheDroidsYoureLookingFor
14/10/12 13:54 GMT
This comment has been removed for legal reasons.

PusBrooks
14/10/12 14:40 GMT
This comment has been removed for legal reasons.

MrWhite
14/10/12 14:45 GMT
I am now getting very angry with you. I am resending this message once more: When will you release the 2011 acoustic take of 'Cougar Hearts' live at the Electric Tank studios? I have found a bootleg copy, but the quality is sub par and the vocal track is distorted. Is there a clean version available?

16 October
I can't believe what happened to me today. I was in the supermarket buying a packet of chicken escalopes for dinner. The woman behind the

till, I don't know what you call her, she says to me: Are you paying for these chicken escalopes with the money from your racist song? I told her it was not racist and she should call the manager. She said you don't want to talk to my manager. I said I don't care. So the manager comes and he is a black man. Right, I have nothing against black men AS YOU ALL KNOW, but I wanted to continue with my complaint. I said the woman called me a racist. She said she didn't call me a racist, but she said my song was racist. The manager apologised for the woman calling my song racist. But he was kind of smiling. I wanted to say F. YOU. I really wanted to say F. YOU. But I didn't say F. YOU. Because that's not the kind of person I am.

Comments

BuckFast
16/10/12 13:23 GMT
You call her a cashier.

17 October
I don't usually use this blog to write personal things. But I have another story and it is sad and I want to tell this to you, my friends, the fans and even to the people who don't like me and look on this blog to confirm why they don't like me and want to laugh at me, because the sound of their laughter drowns out having to THINK and having to CARE.

Anyway I wanna tell you about what happened. It is to do with my girl. First, let me give you some history.

I met Sal at the Hop and Bark pub in Homerton seven years ago. A great little venue. They had an open mike night every Wednesday for aspiring songwriters. I was still in college and not knowing who I was or what I wanted to be. All I was sure of was that I was put on this planet to sing.

It was a competition. If you won, you got to do an extra set at the end of the evening, plus two free drinks. She was behind the bar. Me and the guitar knocked out a couple of tunes. I spied her from the stage. She was fitter than I ever thought fit could be. Black bobbed hair. Dark eyes. Beautiful eyeliner. Really dark and exciting. She was checking me out too, or so I thought. But when you're onstage, you think everyone in the crowd is into you. Afterwards I went to the bar and positioned myself so I was sure it was her who would serve me.

I remember the exact words we first spoke to each other.

"You're too big for this dive," she said.

"So are you," I said.

"You calling me fat?" she said.

"I'm calling you great."

"It sounds like a kind word for fat."

I thought I had f-ed up. So I went to sit on my own with my pint. I had a couple of other beers, but I didn't buy them from her. At the end of the night, I won the competition. So I went back on stage.

Before I began my victory set, I said: "This one is for the girl in black behind the bar. If heaven is a pub, she'll be serving the drinks."

You got the biggest cheer of that evening, Sal. And in my heart every night since, even when I am away, on the nights I go on stage and the crowd is heaving, you always get a louder cheer from me.

It hasn't been easy. It's hard for a girl when you are going steady with a public figure like myself. The last 12 months on tour have seen some challenges. I won't go into these right now. But things happen when you are a famous person working so closely with a bunch of people 24/7.

So last night we were sitting in the pub and I was talking to her about all this shit I was getting from the media and from the people in the supermarket. Anyway, she turned to me and said "I am leaving you."

At first I could not say anything. So I asked her if it was because of the scandal. She said that no, it was not because of the scandal. I said I know I have been a bit crazy these days. She said that was not a problem, she would have told me earlier, but I always seemed to be so angry, that she did not want to add to my problems. She decided a long time ago that it was over. It had been over since the tour began.

"What must I do to get you back?" I asked her.

She said she had to go outside for a cigarette.

Comments

GBdaBest
17/10/12 12:05 GMT
I. Am. In. Tears.

SpockTease
17/10/12 12:23 GMT
You are the spirt of the true England.

VladimirPutin
17/10/12 14:02 GMT
This comment has been removed for legal reasons.

MrWhite
17/10/12 14:45 GMT
I am asking one more time - when will you release the 2011 acoustic take of 'Cougar Hearts' live at the Electric Tank studios? I have found a bootleg copy, but the quality is sub-par and the vocal track is distorted. Is there a clean version available? Shouldn't you be answering me, Mr Brooks? It's

ALL ABOUT THE FANS, eh?

19 October

Sorry I've been out of the picture. Slept for 25 hours straight. I dreamt of chasing rainbows across a metal hill packed with purple buttercups. Edgar Allen Poe was there drinking bourbon, while a litter of black cats crawled on his lap and shoulders. The sun was setting. But the sky was a clear blanket of red. Then the night came. A bright red night. Then a bright red day. It was beautiful and ugly at the same time. Since then, I've been obsessing about a lot of things - life and stuff. 'England' is still riding high the top ten, but what does it mean, guys? What does it all mean, eh?

Comments

SpockTease

19/10/12 17:06 GMT

Life be bad.

22 October

Sal moved all her stuff out while I was in Derby doing a gig. She took her furniture, her cutlery and pots and pans and the TV. The house is virtually empty now. I realised I don't have many belongings. All I had was hers. Except for a bunch of records.

Now I order take-away Chinese or Vietnamese. I drink a decent bottle of red. One that costs over a tenner. I put a disc on the turntable, watch the stylus hit the vinyl and then stare at the ceiling, at the blank wall or at the lamps on the street outside. I lie in my living room on the carpet. I look at all the dimples in the fabric where her stuff once stood. It's all scuffed up with a few tears and needs changing.

Comments

FlooringGoldmine
22/10/12 19:56 GMT
Discount Laminate Flooring
Factory prices laminate flooring at heavy discounts of $0.49 per square foot.
Save up to 67 per cent on retail and 33 per cent on wholesale!
We deliver anywhere!
www.discountflooringexcellentdeal.com

26 October
The song is still selling. We've slipped down the charts to number 23. The song is still banned. The news reports have slacked off a bit. But now and again I get a few comments from people on the street. I explain to everyone that my song has a liberal heart. But no one seems to believe me. Maybe they do believe me, but they say they don't because they don't like the fact that I'm successful. That I'm rich. Yet I tell them how I try to give my money away. I tell them that it means nothing to me. But the causes I love don't want my money. So what can I do? I've decided to forget it all. To even stop writing these messages. I have gone back to what I am best at. Just a poor balladeer trying to sing the news. And I've written a song. Call it a kind of sign-off song for this blog. I thought about writing about how great England is. About how inclusive it is. But I couldn't. So I rewrote my hit. I will only play this version from now on. The same music. But with new words. What more can I do? What more can an artist do?

CHORUS:

England doesn't want you
When you sing these words
England doesn't want you
When you sing these words

VERSE:

England hate you when
You're making a stand
England hate you when
You defend England

(CHORUS)

VERSE:
England hate your lyrics
Chorus, verse and break
All England wanna do
Wanna do is hate

(CHORUS)

BREAK:

All England wanna do
All England wanna do
All England wanna do

Is hate
Hate you when you truth
Hate you when you lie
Hate you when you use
Your right to reply
Hate you when you're top
Hate you when you're low
Hate you when you got
Nowhere else to go

Comments

There are no comments

Joanna Campbell

After launching her writing career with the Bristol Short Story Prize 2010, Joanna Campbell from Gloucestershire is so grateful to have another story in this year's anthology.

She has been shortlisted three times for the Bridport and Fish Prizes. Her collection of stories reached the shortlist of the 2012 Flannery O'Connor Award. This year she came second in the William Trevor/Elizabeth Bowen International Short Story Competition and won the local prize in the Bath Short Story Award.

Last year her novel about Berlin reached the final ten in a Cinnamon Press competition. She is currently writing a new novel and a short story collection.

Wind And Water

I said to Pa how if the invisible man posted a letter into Mercy's Mercantile today, he'd be seen for sure. Every tractor is idle. Every cow is lowing to be milked. Every man is searching. Every woman is waiting at a window. The school won't open other than for search parties to gather.

My feet slap across the flat land by the sea, through the salicornia growing in the salt, whipping at my legs in the wind. It looks like fire when it turns red. A sea of fire makes no sense, but it sure looks that way. I'm walking through wet flame. The plant has the tiniest leaves, but until you're close up and looking you'd think it was just grass.

The letter in my pocket stings my leg, rubbing it under my shorts. Pa says to post it into the shop when there's no one around. I have to look over my shoulders, twice or thrice times, turn right around and then act like I'm just having a regular play with a good pebble from the grass, throwing, skimming, clanging it against the shop.

We're always smashing stones at the corrugated iron. We don't make marks. Just noise. The kind boys make for crack, not for people to turn and look. I turned eighteen in the summer so I guess throwing stones belongs to some other time. Glad I got the chance again.

I wish Clem was walking with me. He makes me braver. Crackpot, is what Pa calls it. Clem wouldn't know how to post a letter without anyone seeing. There's a lot of movement when you post a letter. Think of all you do. You stop. You squat if the slot is way down near the kickboard. You near enough need to lie on your belly to slide anything into the shop's slot. Then you have to pull your hand free of the flap before it snaps you like a fly-trap from Venus. In winter-gloves it takes a moment.

I haven't done it yet. I've thought about it first. And that's what Clem can't do. Thinking. Looking close. Eyeing up the breadth of a leap from the sea-fence so you don't get yourself caught in the mire. Gauging the direction your pebble will take, making sure it hits the metal, not the glass pane that's too damn smeared for me to call it a window.

Pa said to use cunning and daring. He said life's a waste if you don't. No one can learn them to you at school. He's relying on me, he says. He says to look deep in his eyes and see the truth. And the only truth I need to know is that I'm loved.

Pa's the only living soul I got. And family is the salt of the earth. You stay with what you have, even if there's just the one. And he's grey-grizzled and creaking. No matter. You stay where you're loved.

Pa drove the tractor when he was blind drunk. He drove it off furrow. He drove it where a barrow of frozen earth marked my sister's grave. Tractor caught the edge of the barrow. It ploughed through Ma. She was grieving there. She was tired.

She heard it coming at her through the dark. She heard the thunder in the earth. She was my mother and she was lame. She dropped to the ground because there was nowhere else. She was tired and lame, my mother. The wheel that's taller than me rolled over her head.

The trial's soon. They know he's going nowhere. They watch him, but he's just an old man in mourning. And they know he won't leave me.

When Pa's locked away, the plan is for Clem's family to sop me up like sucking an oyster from its shell. There's thirteen boys and girls in that family, last count. His brothers kick out in their greasy sleep. I don't want to talk in mine.

Wish I was walking with Clem right now. There's red faces calling him and whacking the marshes with sticks, but I'm alone. I wait. My breath's hard.

A heron watching a tide-pool is also watching me. He lives in the creek waiting for fish to emerge from the marsh when the tide changes. Mummichogs and grass shrimp crouch in a pool of marsh water for the tide to go out. A diamondback terrapin is laying its eggs, one eye turned toward me. Alligators are basking behind me in fresher brine. Their heads turn at every move I make. Even just a sigh.

I walk on. This is a time for being bold. If I walk to the shop like any other day and post the letter as if it's the most normal thing in the world anyone can do, no one will notice. No stealth. Just walk up brisk, quick look over the shoulders, maybe thrice times, and do it.

The shop's doing business today. Fifty folk could go missing round here and still Mercy's Mercantile would be open for the world and his wife to see her fat old dugs leaning squat on the counter.

Mind you, she has kept the door closed and clapped the flimsy screen over. Ain't no flies at this time of year, but Mercy wishes to show respect for the family of a missing boy. A kind of mourning. Everyone knows that a missing person round here is oft-times never seen again. Lost to the marsh, crusted with salt way down where the small fishes bite all day and all night.

Mercy, she misses nothing. But today with the screen across, she only has the window. And it ain't seen a leather for months. If I creep from the back and round the side, I can throw myself to the ground, push the letter through the darned slot and be gone. She might think the wind had high-whistled the way it does, squealing right around her steel shack of a shop. And I can hear her saying, "My, I hope Clemmy has a coat about his back if he's hunkered out in this all night long." And I can see her take a suck on her cigarillo and tug at her bodice to ease the strain while she leans and waits and catches sight of the letter we made from a paper-bag, a thin white square on her floor.

I don't know why I want Clem here. He's a wretch, the worst coward I know. Pa says we can put our hands in Clem's mind like we dip them in the dish-washing water, scooting things about, swirling and swishing, getting the stuck dirt off and bringing them out clean. And Clem would scarce notice.

But when you feel alone, anyone counts. Clem's my friend, but he'd mess this up if he stood beside me now. He'd wet hisself like he does in the night. Wind and water, that's what Clem is. Wind and water. Like this place, only without its silent sucking strength. Without its hidden eyes watching, its hidden heart beating.

Anyways, if Clem was here, he wouldn't be where he is now.

The search is sterner, hands and arms sweeping trees aside, shouts and barks circling in the wind. But the hope it had at the get-go is flagging. Clem is slow, people are saying. He could be sauntering anywhere under that great sky full of milk up there. Or he could be way below the foggy water that waits to take a soul down. I see them looking up. And I see them looking down. That's how's I know what folks are saying.

Pa's hands are busy now. I can feel it. I'm a thousand paces from our house, but I know it. I stride to the shop. I can feel Mercy's hands waiting for me to come by. They paw me in back of the shop when I bring in the marrows. Pa and I grow them, great shining fruits of the soil. And yams with their dirt-jackets. Cut them and warm yourself on the glow.

I bring them for her to sell in the shop and she goes roaming all over me. Fresh from the earth today, Miss Mercy, I tell her. That's not me, mind. Just you check out what I have in my sack, Miss Mercy. She laughs some.

She don't give over for a full minute. And she still touches me. Means nothing by it. Loveless place, her shop, she says. Says she has to git it where she can.

Three glances over my shoulder and I'm down. I push the letter in. I think Pa knows it's there. I can feel him unstrapping the ties, peeling off the gag. And there's Clem with the words scrambling in his head. We just have to hope they come out the right way. Only way to get truth out is to put truth in.

I washed the scarf that made the gag. Pa took it off to give him grits for breakfast. We let the butter melt right in. That's the way Clem eats it if he ever gits the chance. He said he'd stay there, bound though he was, just for the grits. He smiled in our chair with the strips of flannel and sheet pressing and gripping his wrists and ankles hard. That's how his brain works. It's about now. The past is only in his head for a moment.

Pa's telling him again how things were that day. And Clem will nod and agree and say the right thing.

I walk around the shop the other way; quiet, smooth paces. The wind and I are gliding together, free and unchecked. No one is here. Mercy is humming inside, clattering open the jar of chewing-nuts that have cost her all but three teeth. The counter creaks under her weight.

People say she's Clem's true mother. She lived with her Grampa til he drank hisself to shrivelling. He was nothing but veins, they say. People round here say things all the time. They say her babe came one night after a ten-month of being inside her. Small, they said, but the head swollen like it was a creature from another place. So swollen that Mercy's scream could be heard right down as far as the fresh water. A mermaid, they say, shivered on the seabed that night.

No one counts the folk at Clem's. No one does a reckoning of how much love's left in his mother's heart. She takes in anyone lost. In that bed that slants and dips, the bed where Clem and all the rest sleep, who knows which belong by blood? Clem's mother loves them all. They're all hers.

By now, Mercy will be seeing the letter. As I walk away to the marsh, she is picking it up, her breath coming hard as she stoops, her old stays crackling and her hair hanging over her face. I stand still, let the crows settle, wait for the air to clear. And I swear I can hear her unfold the paper and run her finger under the words. Might take her some time. The chewing-nuts might have to sit on her tongue while her mouth gapes at what she's reading.

I'll hear her scream. And if I wait long enough, I'll hear the whistles and the shouts that awaken the search for Clem. He's hiding 'cause he was fearing of the truth, was what he wrote. And the sea could take him, wash his shame. He's ready to be swept away, he wrote. He wrote the words hisself. He was scared of the face of truth.

Aren't all of us damn scared of it? I'm scared of what will happen to Clem now. Driving a tractor that don't belong to you and mowing down an innocent woman praying at the graveside. Letting the world think Pa was at the wheel. Letting Pa save a boy's hide, shouldering the blame to spare his future from shame.

I watched Pa outside at night, not sleeping while he mourned his wife, just as if he'd been halved under that wheel too. Not sleeping 'cause he feared dying in a jail cell. And I wasn't having it. I was having the truth, I told him one night when the sky was an old web coming down and the sea-pie birds had given over smashing shells for the day.

We watched an oyster reef glinting silver under the moon. I could hear it rocking in the swell. The water stirred, clicking the oyster shells together in their gentle way to make a home for barnacles and hook-mussels.

That reef had made the sea between tides a huge old hide-out for those little creatures gripping the oysters, nestling safe in the nooks between them. I could feel the suction keeping them all fast and true, hiding them from the croakers and hardheads slithering just below the surface. Sometimes Pa and me try to catch the weakfish, but they live up to their name most times. Their mouth muscles are so damn slack, slacker and softer than Mercy's Pa's when the bottle was pouring itself into his throat, that the hook rips clean out soon as it catches on. We think we're damn near about to take one, but they wrench free every damn time.

That night we listened to the fish dreaming, sitting on the bank under that great sky and I told him I wouldn't let him tell an untruth to save Clem.

"He might own the truth if we ask him to," I said. My words dropped like godwit chicks drowning. I knew no one could force him to speak out.

I felt impatient, wondering why Pa was waiting, just waiting to be taken away. I felt him keep on coming to my bedside in the night with tears in his old voice, whispering things in my head until the sky was down and the sea was up. He churned up my head with talk of my mother until I cried hard in my pillow like no boy should cry.

But one night the plan was made. Pa was different, like he'd reached the end of a long task and was sitting back, sighing with pleasure at the ease his mind was taking.

"We'd need to coax him in, feed him whisky, tie him up. Wash his brain into confessing without no one knowing we've done it, Pa," I said, these words sliding out, already made and shaped and as strong as the green gutweed mats smacking over the summer mudflats.

He nodded, lighting his pipe and making those popping sounds with it in the old way he used to do before my mother died. As if he'd reached peace inside himself and his love for me wound with his smoke way up into the trees, like it held our secret.

I knew he'd say we could do this, we could get Clem to speak up and let an old man live in peace with his grieving heart. I knew his answer like I'd already heard it, as if the wind had whispered it into my poor lamenting head at night when I slept. I knew Clem's jaw would loosen and the words we drummed in would roll right back out.

"We could do it, Jason," Pa said right then and there under the sour night sky, puffing his smoke right up into it and watching it vanish.

They find Clem by the shore. His confession, scribbled in his own writing on a bag from Mercy's shop and held in Mercy's hands as they once held poor Clem himself when he came from her belly, sure did make Mercy scream.

She made all the searchers swarm to the sea where he was sat on a rock, a-watching the tide and a-waiting. Just like we told him.

We told Clem they'd go easy. Coming clean was the right thing. He was a lad and he didn't have all his head. Parts were missing, we said. Didn't he know his blood was the wrong mix? we asked him.

He screwed up his eyes at that. Like making apple pie with salt 'stead of sugar, we said. And he nodded, knowing they were two things that didn't go together.

Yep, he said, he felt sometimes like he were a strange old brew. He nodded with the wisdom of it all, with the dawning truth. And we said that made him different, even maybe special. And that did it.

We watched him write the confession in silence, save for the pen squawking on the paper.

The sheriff takes him in. People bring gifts to Pa all day. For the first time they all say they knew he was an innocent man. They lay their pots of jelly and flagons of berry cordial on the doorstep. We stack them in the cellar, in the cool. They stand one on top of another, like a monument to the truth, a symbol of what is right, a tombstone for my poor dead mother.

I hope the nights settle now. I haven't slept well since the day the tractor went off furrow.

I'll miss Clem, but he's a boy and they might not keep him shut away for good and all. Me, I'm eighteen. They'd have locked me in the dark that never ends. I'd be a young man rotting like a brown cider-apple in the long grass.

Think of that, Pa had whispered in the dark all those nights. Think of your wasted life. He kept me strapped to the bed with his belts pressing me flat. It was merciless. I wet the sheets. It felt hot and cold both, like a sea of fire. But it was safe. I wasn't going anywhere held down like that with Pa breathing the new truth in my ear, telling me what Clem did and how he took the wheel. How I kept saying no, he shouldn't.

A sea of fire makes no sense until some soul says it sure looks that way.

And Pa whispered on into the night until the truth didn't sound like the truth any more, until it was almost invisible and made of wind and water.

Ric Carter

Originally from Bury in North-West England, Ric Carter lives in the Channel Island of Guernsey where he shares a flat with his girlfriend, his cat and a small library. He publishes on his own website (Digestive Press), has produced several handmade chapbooks and has had work featured in various places online. To date he has written over 200 short stories and has no plans to stop soon. He also enjoys walking, eating biscuits and eating biscuits whilst walking.

The Standing Still

The trips to see doctors, to see psychologists, the trips to the military facility. The grey hairs. The nights when Mr and Mrs Nilsen finally get home, exhausted, wide-eyed and wide-minded, stretched chock-full of being told one thing then another. The way they are adamant that they can cope with it all, the way it slowly becomes clear that they could not, would not. The way the house quickly progresses through dusty, dirty, out of control. The four children left on their own, Lord-of-the-Flies-ing it out, their feet smacking up and down the stairs, their shrill screams, Moira throwing Adam against the wall as they rowed, Beth crying because. And the way Soren could always find a quiet spot in the house to sit and make her boxes, hundreds of boxes, tiny soundproof boxes that were too small to fit anything that could possibly need peace and quiet. The fact that this could not be celebrated, the way they are terrified she might turn out the same way as Tobias.

Tobias blindfolded, the doctor standing behind him, Mr and Mrs Nilsen seated on the other side of the room. The only clock in the room taken down and disarmed, the tick-tocking stopping. Tests lasting hours, lasting days, stretching out over weeks. The doctor assuring them nothing is wrong, there is nothing to worry about. Second and third and fourth opinions, a repeat prescription of consultations. Hauling Tobias from specialist to specialist, Tobias approaching each diagnosis with a kind of weary amusement. His heart monitored, his brain scanned, his blood tested. Appointments with psychologists, the psychologists trying to work out if it is a trick or an affliction, Tobias repeating the same answers he has been giving for months, growing bored of the attention.

Occasional trips to Pizza Portrait on the way home. Tobias pulling a silly face for the camera, and then laughing like any twelve-year-old boy when his food arrives and it looks just like him.

The clocks going forward, Tobias barely missing a beat. Trotting out the time for whichever professional is asking – Tuesday, 17:24 and 39 seconds, 14 minutes and 13 seconds since last time. Or 853 seconds. The summer unstoppable.

Mr and Mrs Nilsen asking him the same questions, then turning and asking the professionals. Is he counting all the time, is that how he does it? And the doctors saying that perhaps he is counting, subconsciously, or perhaps it is part of his brain, a part that no one else has ever had before. The doctors saying that they are on the verge of giving up, of accepting that Tobias is just a thing that is, a twelve-year-old boy with an unusual skill.

The clocks going back, Tobias barely missing a beat. The military taking an interest, keen to see what they can make out of him, threatening to take Tobias away. The military saying it is for the good of the nation. The military taking Tobias away.

Mr Nilsen storming home, crashing through the house, destroying Soren's boxes one by one in complete silence.

A room in the military facility. Tobias being given lessons, being taken outside for exercise. The generals testing him every day, tests designed not to diagnose him but to improve him, to sharpen his instincts. His skill redefined as a superpower. Tobias turning thirteen, Tobias knowing exactly when this occurs. Mr and Mrs Nilsen visiting but no sign of his feral siblings.

Their regular visits suddenly stopping. Tobias knowing exactly how long it is between visits.

Time passing, seconds hammering along, minutes, hours, days following. Tobias' tests changing. Military scientists asking him to see what he can do, to see if he can stop time, reverse time, make time go faster, to amend instead of observe. Pressure. Generals screaming at him, Tobias straining, desperate to please, the ticking of the passing seconds growing only louder.

The trips to the Citizens Advice Bureau, the trips to see their Member of Parliament, the anti-military campaign groups. The grey hairs. The handing out leaflets on street corners, on buses, putting them through letterboxes. This is what happened to our son. Help us. Mr and Mrs Nilsen coming home late at night, charcoal-eyed and frozen-minded, exhausted and ignored. Hope dwindling, a sense of senselessness. The other children carrying on, organising themselves, forming dictatorships and staging coups and counter-coups, the house existing in a state of perpetual revolution, and only Soren finding spaces in which to rebuild her little boxes.

The clocks going forward, Tobias barely missing a beat. Time weighing heavy now, a sense of his own mortality. More tests, the generals becoming dispirited, knowing Tobias can be of use to them, not knowing how.

Being moved to another facility. Being moved in the middle of the night and knowing exactly when. Not knowing where. Tobias being introduced to Lucille. Lucille stating coldly the exact temperature of the room. Tobias being introduced to Barney. Barney picking up a pencil and telling Tobias its exact weight. Tobias and Lucille and Barney discussing the books and games they are given to keep them entertained. Being aware of the time and the season and the weight of the world, being unable to affect a single thing.

The fact that Mr and Mrs Nilsen spend whole days campaigning outside the military facility. The fact that they do not know they are outside the wrong military facility. The fact that no one is taking any notice anyway. Going home to find that their four remaining children insist on carrying on with their little lives. Mr Nilsen smashing Soren's soundproof boxes, taking her by the shoulders, shaking her. Soren leaving through her bedroom window in the middle of the night.

The summer exploding with war. Rumours circulating that the military have special weapons, children who can manipulate time, children who can lift impossible weights, children who could boil a whole country alive if the generals gave the order. People marching through the capital. Mr Nilsen being badly beaten at an anti-war demonstration.

Nothing ending quickly, nothing neatly tidied away. The clocks going back, Tobias barely missing a beat. The beat of bombs on the TV set. The clocks going forward, Tobias barely missing a beat. The beat of Mr Nilsen's heart, Mrs Nilsen sitting at her husband's bedside. The clocks going back, Tobias barely missing a beat. Quick on her feet, Soren scavenging for food, finding quiet places, making quick and accurate folds, forming little soundproof boxes. Tobias constantly reminded that time is passing, that it is moving on again before he has the chance to finish his thought.

Knowing the exact second, the minute, the hour, the date when he is moved again, once more in the dead of night. The night dead but still ticking. Being blind to the directions the van is taking. Van, plane, van. Being alone. Being given a bag of clothes and a stash of cash, being kicked out of the van. Blinking in the sunlight. Finding himself in a city he does not recognise. Realising that he is in a different time zone, somewhere East. Choosing a meal for himself, wondering what to do next.

Finding digs, reading about the war, growing his hair long, dying it copper, walking in the park. Time passing gently, the booming of war thousands of miles away, the ticking in his head, Tobias moving on to the next city, thinking about home, reading about the war, reading the rumours that the military has secret weapons, Tobias not having the money to get home, unsure if he actually wants to get home, barely able to form a thought before the next moment is ticking past, ticking past, whole days spent lying in bed or in the park, the seconds ticking too loud, the sense of his mortality too obvious. The clocks going forward, Tobias wincing as he barely misses a beat.

Mr Nilsen passing away slowly in his hospital bed, the lines blurring around the exact time of his demise. Mrs Nilsen creeping home, Moira pregnant, Adam detained, Beth taken away to be cared for. Soren criss-crossing the country, leaving little pockets of silence in her wake.

Moving on, working her way through the cities, looking for her brother. Keeping one eye on news of the war across the sea, the booming and the blasting, wishing she could make the world quieten down. Searching the cities she finds herself in, filling a satchel with fruit from understaffed market stalls, sleeping under bridges. Hanging out with the bums, stilling their anxieties. Watching the witches swimming with their inflatable cats on a Christmas Day, the stray dogs practising yoga in the park, the peace wizards busking. Soren making little boxes, spreading them out in front of her, selling them to strangers. Asking questions.

Tobias in a new city, meeting peaceniks in the park, falling in love, being mistaken for a girl, staying up all night to try and escape the counting. Counting nonetheless. Moving on again, not staying still, stopping there, staying still, hoping to out-run time, or perhaps trick time into passing him by. Mixing it up, bobbing and weaving, trying to confuse either the universe or his own mind. Adjusting the chemical make-up of his brain to drown out the relentless- Detoxing to flush from his system the neverending- Moving on to another new city, stumbling across a military homecoming, glaring at the soldiers, throwing things at the soldiers, getting himself arrested. Generals saying, hey aren't you-

Another military facility. Tobias beaten, broken, barely fed. His head shaved. Left staring at blank walls. Unable to stop time, unable to stop the war.

Generals bringing in a young boy, six or seven or eight years old. Tobias lifting his head to see. The general's hand on the young boy's shoulder. The young boy laughing, his eyes tight and tiny, too close together. The general nodding to the young boy, a single, swift nod.

The young boy staring, making a machine gun sound with his mouth, rat-a-tat-a-tatting. The seconds speeding up, the metronome in Tobias' head getting faster, 100bpm, 200bpm, 300bpm. Tobias feeling the influx of time on a cellular level, feeling his soul ageing. Getting faster and faster. Tobias' head jerking backwards as the clocks go back, like going over a speed bump. The ticking becoming a wall of noise. The young boy stopping and starting again, making a different noise, now time running backwards, a whole new sound in Tobias' head. Speeding up, slowing again. Stopping. The young boy stopping time just exactly where they had started, and Tobias' head blank for the first time ever, a blank canvas, a beautiful blank canvas.

The war trembling on.

Tobias allowed to leave – scared, broken, beaten. The seconds ticking by. A stranger asking if he has the time, Tobias giving the stranger a precise answer, the stranger laughing as he says thanks. Knowing exactly how long it is now since he first admitted his talent, was taken to the doctors, etcetera, etcetera. Thinking about the general and the little boy laughing when time started up again. Finding himself a quiet spot to sit and think it over. His thoughts chased on. The sun hanging high in the sky.

The clocks going back, Tobias barely missing a beat. Looking down at his feet, seeing a collection of tiny boxes spread across the pavement, remembering something. Time tricking him, time feeling like it is slowing to treacle thick. Soren looking up, a little dishevelled, an air of peace.

Exclaiming, staring, disbelieving, jumping, hugging, crying, smiling, talking, eating dinner in a cafe.

The volume turned up on the television in the corner. A news bulletin beginning. A crowd forming, a realisation dawning that something important is going to happen, everyone craning their necks to see the set. No one giving their opinion, everyone knowing it is too late for that, being too small and alone for words.

Being glad that they are not on their own. Just wanting to see. Everyone crowding around together.

Tobias and Soren not paying attention to the news. Soren putting the fingers of her left hand on her brother's right temple, putting the fingers of her right hand on her brother's left temple. Tobias not looking, not seeing the boy, six or seven or eight years old, there on the screen. Everyone in the cafe crowding around the television to see.

Mrs Nilsen watching the news on her own, thinking about her lost children, hoping they are ok.

Everyone in the cafe crowding around the television to see. Stretching, straining, gasping.

Maybe one person turning to look at the two children sitting in the window.

Time stopping.

Ruth Corkill

Ruth Corkill was born in London in 1993 and is working towards her Masters in Physics at Victoria University of Wellington in New Zealand. She was a student at the International Institute of Modern Letters and her work has previously appeared in *the Dominion Post, Hue and Cry,* and *JAAM.* A visit to Rochester, Minnesota in 2012 inspired *Med City* and she has just returned to Wellington from a trip to the Kinabatangan region of Borneo. Although she loves to travel, her favourite place to be and think is Abel Tasman National Park, New Zealand.

Med City

You cannot leave the hospital. This is Med City, it is written on the taxis. The Kingdom of the sick that rises out of the cornfields. We flew in this morning and already the rest of the world seems unreal. When they called for passengers to Rochester the old, the decrepit, the deformed, my mother and myself separated out of the crowd and queued up to board. We played a game on the aeroplane; Patient, Relative or Doctor. At Rochester international airport there is a stack of wheelchairs next to the trolleys. In the hotel lobby there is a wig shop and a pharmacy. The bathroom has brown tiles on the floor that creep right into the corners and up the walls. Billie's voice doesn't own this space; she mutters Gloomy Sunday from my speaker on the toilet lid, the tiles steal her heat and the heat of the bath. James said it was the old lady music that made me so tired. I turn the hot water on and Billie disappears in the static of the pipes. Do you want a bath? You will be covered in road grease. They bury their dead in the cornfields.

I try changing the song. But there is no denying Rochester Minnesota, Med City. This city is a transplants ward, a chemo ward, outpatients, reception, waiting room, that loom over the hotels and restaurants. For feeding and cleaning the patients. And beyond are the factory farmed, genetically engineered corn fields rustled by the hot wind off the Nevada

Desert. The Mississippi flows slowly here, there is nowhere to go. Try telling it apart from the lakes when you're up close. It seemed that we drove through endless corn fields to get here.

And you were initially diagnosed seven years ago, is that correct?

Yes

And is that when you began your current medication regime? Or has that been altered?

The meals sure focus on size in Minnesota, huh? Great steaming plates of calories that slide off the bones of the bald men teetering at their tables. Gluten free, low GI, low fat, sugar free, suitable for diabetics, dairy free. Easily digested. Here the undignified, dead to all who hangs onto another month, day, meal. How long have you been at the clinic? There is a nurse without a uniform in the hotel dining room. She moves amongst the tables dispensing plates and mothering. Perhaps you have to be a nurse first to be a waitress here. How are you going sir? You're done? Do you want me to put that in a box for you or are you done done? That man looks dead. The Grand has a wonderful swimming pool, heated for hydrotherapy. I would die if couldn't swim every day.

How do you want the light?

Off.

How do you want the door?

Closed.

Following denial of allergy and review of potential side effects and complications including but not necessarily limited to infection, allergic reaction, local tissue breakdown, systemic effects of corticosteroids, elevation of blood glucose, injury to soft tissue and/or nerves and seizure, the patient indicated understanding and agreed to proceed.

The revolving doors spit you onto the sterile streets of Rochester. I saw the trucks this morning, spraying antiseptic. Here a motorised pile of contorted limbs buzzes his way through the midsummer. There is a boy with callipers sprouting from his sneakers. A tiny child, he sways violently, and the sneakers have red lights that flash with each laboured step. Such fine shoes, I say, they are very cool. He smiles upside down, the way you do when someone says what they shouldn't. But I am right, and as he averts his eyes he gives his foot another tap, and the red lights glitter in the surface of the callipers. I don't have anything else to say. James is better with children than I am. Do you see anyone who is not a nurse a doctor a relative a patient? What are you doing here? You are neither dead nor dying. I am one of so many sick.

Do you need anything?

Just go to bed.

These foolish things are out of keeping now

And I am sick to the heart, and tired always of creaking and limping between the ward beds, of this illness I will die waiting out, that will not kill me. My heart and lungs are healthy. Though my muscles will waste around the bones that will not carry them, carbon and crumbling into the daylight.

There is a restaurant two blocks away from the hospital buildings, reserved by distance for those who can make it. It's the only place in town that's a little grubby and doesn't play show tunes. I check my emails while my mother checks tomorrow's appointments. You have to be at pathology at 8am tomorrow. They want more bloods. We have fish and wild rice for dinner, and I talk about the email from James. He thinks we should buy wigs. But the real taxis of Med City moan past. The white van that took the bed in the next room and turned it on its end. Left it in the corridor stripped of sheets and laid bare. And the taxi lights flash red and blue and the moan becomes a howl. At least the ambulance doesn't have far to go. It's only two blocks.

There is a man at the next table. He has come from Brighton and is surely old enough to remember parties silenced by sirens. There is a war on, men die every day, bombs are dropped on civilians. His son struggles with his spoon, struggles to make words of sound. He must have a head injury. His young wife and his parents try to pretend this is just another dinner in another foreign town. Charming decor, I like the defibrillator especially. I remember seven years ago when Andrea and I were walking towards her mother's car and she said, "Please don't talk about your joints when mum asks you how you are. She thinks you just complain all the time. There is always something else wrong." I stare at the son at the other table. At least people believe him, he is so obviously crippled.

Was I always such a bitter person?

In the pool I could be anywhere. Under the water in silence and darkness. I could be underwater anywhere. Then I break the surface and a man without legs is easing himself out of his wheelchair. James and I used to go aqua jogging twice a week as part of my rehabilitation.

She may have mild sleep disordered breathing given her oropharyngeal anatomy. It will be necessary to rule out any other primary sleep disorders which could result in restlessness and fragmented sleep and hence worsen her chronic pain symptoms. She will try to take a hypnotic agent at midnight.

I met a girl in hospital. Her body breathed in surges, waves crashing on a beach. And she was so thin, her ribs scraped my thighs, she pushed my legs aside and made my mangled hip moan. Heat that made my back arch as her tongue searched. But it was a dream, and now when she sees me and sits quietly beside me in the waiting room I turn and talk to someone else. The man next to me is wearing loafers without socks. James told me once that only creepy old men don't wear socks. But this man is young, and his only reason for being here is a cast on his arm.

The middle-aged woman waiting for consultation with the orthopaedic surgeon had never left Wisconsin before. The pager buzzes red and blue, arteries and veins are what you are, please take a seat and they will call you from door A. Lift your knee for me, we'll need you to change into a robe, you can leave on your panties and it's just a simple shift with domes at the back. Is that painful? Right here? What brings you to Rochester?

Does anyone come to Rochester not for the clinic?

No, not really.

It is darkness, and I do not know you in this searing, blinding pain

Your face is too bright. They have cut off my limbs, they are in the wrong places, inside each other, entangled and shattered. I see through the dark, my fingers clawing my skin, tearing it away.

Then when I awake I am pale, and the light touches my skin gently. Every morning for seven years it has been painful to sit up in bed. I bring up bile, bitter and hot in my nose, and the dream is heavy, dragging on the tension in my back. The groaning of my ribcage. Hear the crackling of my sinews, the sting deep and long into my elbow. James brings Star Wars Four, Five, Six, One, Two, and Three to my house. He sits next to me in bed and goes to the kitchen to get water for my pills. He tells my mother to visit her sister for the weekend. He listens after I have stopped making sense and lets me be angry with him. He knows how much it means for me to be at the clinic. I'm seeing the immunologist tomorrow. That's exciting!

On Monday the show tune playlist in the waiting rooms begins again. 42nd street, but without the words, just a piano. I saw 42nd street in San Fran, I know the words and I start giggling in the pathology waiting room, I can't stop giggling it's just too ridiculous. The bald and the creaking turn to marvel at the young hysterical and the piano sings:

I'm young and healthy,

And you've got charms;

It would really be a sin

Not to have you in my arms.

I'm young and healthy,

And so are you;

When the moon is in the sky

Tell me what am I to do?

My sister ate raw food for three years and it cured her cancer.

I know a man who died. We do you know. And remember please how young I am. How you ran in waves and breathed salt spray miles from the corn fields. I know how tired I am. I have no sympathy left for people who become ill at the end of their lives. There is a 70-year-old man who says he cannot work the stock the way he used to. He walks without a stick. The pain is really awful and he has to take aspirin. I don't really bother with aspirin any more.

The acetabular labral tear of the right hip joint has been identified with acetabular retroversion noted radiographically and the tear on the MRI. There is significant surrounding soft tissue damage. It is unclear how much the labral tear versus her underlying migratory intermittent arthralgias are playing into her symptoms.

My mother and I. Do you see our sleepless nights? When the bed sheet burns my skin and she can do nothing. I am her child, nailed to this wheel of screaming and blank eyes. I am so quiet when it is gone, drenched in sweat, the mattress is soggy and sour. She moves me to the lounge so that she can change my bed. I fall into dreams where my symptoms have forms. Someone cracks my skull against the floor. Sounds like concrete. Do we look grey? Sitting in your office, like all the other untouchables who crawl to your door?

I have read the summary Dr Boon sent.

I have read the letter from Dr Broacher.

I see here the notes from Dr Hall and the summary from Dr Boon, but

I'd like to ask you...

Dr Baptise referred you because of your hip, and you have had that MRI and we will talk about those results in a minute but I would also like to get some x-rays of your lower back. It's a fairly risky operation and I think we should avoid it so long as we can manage your symptoms. Best to restrict yourself to cycling and waterborne activities.

Lie here on the bench please. On the metal that seeps cold fingers into your hip. The hip that has been torn and reacts with cysts, that you didn't feel yourself carrying under everything else. Lie on your hip and let me just align your back, get your spine in the right position. In a blue paper gown that rises with comings and goings. The technicians hide while the x-rays jitter about in my ovaries. Giving my children bad spelling and six toes on each foot and an overpowering attraction towards men who wear loafers without socks.

By the time I have children old enough for poor decisions I will be living in a house with handrails in the corridor. Another nurse and another shroud of blue rice paper for the doctor to lay between his hand and my pubic hair while he injects nectar into the joint. With a needle half as long as my forearm. A half cubit, is it steel? James says they may be able to help. He says we will travel in India. But first the burn of anaesthetic, warmth scrabbling off to cling to the fibres of my muscle. The pressure of the ultrasound is enough to hurt that hip. I am lying on my back, my head turned away from the doctor. The pressure of his hand on my thigh, on my stomach, avoiding my crotch like it smells. We've been here ten days, I probably do smell. The pressure of the ultrasound is enough to guide the goliath needle into the soft smooth slope of skin between the jarring of my pelvic bone, my pubic bone and the top of my leg. He eases the needle in, then he has to draw it out and start again. I feel it slip into my flesh. I miss James. I wish he were here to be horrified. Hold me, soothe me afterwards.

On its own it would have been a minor procedure, think of it on its own.

Are you alright?

Yes, I'm fine.

Like a wounded deer my mother tells me. Eyes wide, skin the colour of the veins beneath.

Even with the anaesthetic, says the nurse, it still feels like a needle going into your hip.

Do not bathe or swim for three days, do not submerge the site in water. If the site produces a discharge, begins to smell, or changes colour, consult your health care provider immediately.

How long have you been at the Mayo Clinic?

Ten days.

I have been tired for seven years. Sitting on the 13th floor of the Gonda building, looking at the corn fields beyond Med City. We will do our best to help you manage your symptoms. They bury their dead in the corn fields, and you can taste the morphine in the juice.

Krishan Coupland

Krishan Coupland was born in Southampton, completed his BA at Staffordshire University, and is now studying on the MA Creative Writing course at the University of East Anglia. He runs and edits *Neon Literary Magazine*. His short fiction and poetry has appeared in *Brittle Star, Aesthetica* and *Fractured West*. In 2011 he won the Manchester Fiction Prize for his short story *Days Necrotic*. His website is: www.krishancoupland.co.uk.

Men of the Waste

Around the waste there is Grundy and the clown and the man who comes to fish. The man who comes to fish wears a faded brown body warmer, and pitches his line at the very edge of the scum pond. Grundy watches him, from a distance. Watches as he wrestles the flippering silver bodies from the water and smacks them dead against a rock. Why, Grundy wonders, do the fish keep coming and biting at the line? Don't they smell the blood? What is it to them to see their fellows yanked abruptly skywards, never to return?

Today the man who comes to fish has not caught a single thing. He sits in his little green chair, still as a mannequin, eyes cast into darkness beneath the brim of his cap. Grundy, watching from the opposite shore, from a tangled hide of bushes and leaves, wonders if he is asleep. Perhaps, if he is careful, he can sneak over and search the man's pockets, poke through the canvas bag. Or perhaps he could kill him - smash that cap deep into his head and take everything for himself.

Grundy imagines heaving the body into the scum pond and watching it sink, bubbles rising slowly to the surface as if through jelly. Down there in the dark the fish would turn, dive, set to work with tiny mouths.

On the opposite shore the rod jerks and the man leans forward, evidently awake, to take the strain. Grundy watches as another shining muscled body is lifted from the water. He spits, disappointed.

The clown comes and goes, wandering the waste almost as much as Grundy does. He and Grundy have a cautious appreciation of each other. When they meet they make fleeting eye contact, nod, lips thinning to a semi-smile. They carry on their way without a word. He wears a costume: elaborate rainbow frills dulled by a thick spattering crust of dried mud. Plain white make-up with black stars around the eyes. His face is long and wide-mouthed, the lips ringed by a brown scurf of stubble.

Grundy doesn't watch the clown like he does the man who comes to fish. No interest. The clown doesn't bring meat or shiny things or cigarettes. The clown doesn't bring anything except himself. Grundy has thought about killing him too, in the way he sometimes kills the swamp midges that stray too close to his skin.

Grundy lives in a shack on the far shore of the scum pond. In the morning the wasteland is sunk in mist, the looming lonely shapes of the pylons emerging from it like cresting aeroplanes, calm and cold. Grundy didn't always live in a shack. Once, long ago, he had a house by the sea. People came to him and sat with him in a warm clean room with a fire and a table, books heaped on shelves in uneven humps. There was a cat, he thinks - or perhaps he imagines that bit. But if the cat was real it would sit on the arm of his chair and sleep while he talked with his visitors.

The journey from the house to the shack by the scum pond is one that Grundy cannot fully trace. For a moment this morning when he wakes he knows his mind is gone. He lies there, cold to numbing on a swatch of filthy blankets, listening to the birds clamour outside. He is afraid. Soon enough the fug inside his head will rise again and he will be Grundy, that wild animal, the thing that has no seeming connection to the man who once lived in the house by the sea. Minutes pass. Grundy's eyes glaze and when he wakes again he knows that he is hungry and sickening and cold, and he knows the waste and the scum pond and the clown and the man who comes to fish, and that is all.

After washing in the creek, Grundy must have breakfast. The man who comes to fish sometimes leaves the wimplings of his catch lying on the shore. Else there are the rabbit snares (clumsy loops of wire that most often catch nothing) that Grundy has set down. When both these avenues fail he picks blackberries and sour apples and rips up wet handfuls of cress.

Today he is lucky. The man who comes to fish has left a fair offering of meat. He snaps the fish open with his hands, squeezes out the guts, picks and scrapes until he has the good flesh. Washes the blood away in the scum pond and dries his hands on his own stiff jeans. Blood and scraps of watery flesh stick between his teeth.

He's just finishing when he sees them. Across the scum pond and far down the bank. Two of them: men in yellow hats and yellow jackets. Grundy freezes, then turns slow and burrows down into the brush. He watches. The men have tripods and tools and are measuring things, taking sightings of something Grundy cannot reckon. Council men, more than likely. Above death, Grundy fears the council. Death can be averted, avoided, held back if you're careful. But the council...

He watches, immobile in his hiding place, ignoring the flies that come to feast on fish blood and the beetles that crawl up his back. The council men are loud, unafraid. Grundy can hear their almost-shouted voices quite clearly, but he doesn't understand the words.

On the way back to his shack Grundy meets the clown. He's in among the trees, smothered in mud and so still that Grundy doesn't realise until he's almost upon him. Their eyes meet, both angry, both immediately on guard. They've never been this close before, practically near enough to touch. The smell of gunpowder wafts from the clown in yellow waves. Eyes still on Grundy's he raises a finger to his lips, then points.

There. There among the trees are the council men. Not measuring this time. They're looking at something on the ground. Grundy lowers himself, animal-like, nerves singing. It's one of his snares. One council man is teasing out the wire with the tip of his boot, pulling the loop till it slips over itself. The man beside him mutters something in their weird council language and the others laugh, guttural.

The clown is taut and shaking. And Grundy is shaking too, on the inside, guts roiling with blind hot rage at the men in his waste, breaking his traps. Neither of them move, however. Both know better than that.

The council men stalk around, trampling undergrowth, spitting, one of them lighting up a half-smoked cigarette and then throwing it away minutes later. Eventually they leave, the sound of their voices audible long after they've disappeared through the trees. Grundy and the clown turn to one another. The clown bares his teeth, rolls eyes. Grundy growls in agreement. The council men are bad. Bad and vicious. He watches the clown creep forward to where the men stood, root something up from the dirt and slither back. He holds it out to Grundy; it's the cigarette, still just barely smouldering, a good finger's-width of white paper remaining.

Grundy takes it. Thereafter, he and the clown are friends.

The council men come back the next day, and the day after that. Grundy watches them whenever he can, keeping careful mark of the way they roam the waste. At first some are hesitant, picking through trees as if afraid of bite or poison, staying always a distance from the edge of the scum pond. Soon enough though they lose their fear. Grundy hates them more for it.

Their stamping, laughing, lounging confidence.

The clown watches them too. On occasion Grundy will sight him, his pale face peering from the bushes, or from the canopy of the trees. He is good at hiding. Both are, and so are good at finding hidden things. The council men are oblivious, lost as they are in their measuring and counting.

Twice, Grundy and the clown watch the men together. The clown is good company, silent company. He knows how to lie still and not be seen. And he knows not to talk to Grundy, that they can never understand each other, that it is not worth trying. They are different species, and with this the clown and Grundy are entirely at peace.

Grundy has no plan. For many years Grundy has been beyond the ability to think of the future. He still watches the council men. It is important. The wastes are his and he must know what happens in them, what things and people share his land.

Sometimes in the long hours of hiding, listening to the grunts and snoring words of the invaders, Grundy thinks that he might understand. He recognises the shape of the sounds they make, the civilised tongue. It makes him think of that other place, that old place, warm and soft and buried beneath layers of waste-mud in his mind. The cat that would sleep on the arm of his chair, or not.

A week after they arrive the council men catch the man who comes to fish. Grundy had not thought that this might happen. The man who comes to fish arrives in the early morning, before the light is fully up, and stays only until the middle of the day. The council men come after that and stay until night.

But today, perhaps, the man who comes to fish has stayed longer than usual, or the council men have come earlier. Grundy hears shouting from where he lies in his shack, and snaps awake. The coughs and barks of the council men in anger. Grundy spits, scrambles from his shack into a cold wet mist of rain. It feels silvery on his arms. When he breathes the rain swirls into his lungs like blood in water.

The shouting is coming from the scum pond. Grundy runs at first, then creeps through the last stretch of trees between him and the water. There they are on the opposite shore. Four council men and the man who comes to fish. The council men are shouting, pointing, jabbing the tools they use to measure into the air like dull weapons. The man who comes to fish is red in the face. His little canvas stool lies on its side in the mud, his rod and bucket held protectively behind his back.

Grundy digs around in the coarse slush of the bank until he finds a stone, big and jagged. The muddy coat of it adheres to his fingers, drags on his spindly arm. He watches, anxious not for the man who comes to fish (who, after all, Grundy would happily kill himself if hunger demanded it) but for his wasteland, and his fish, and what might happen if one of the elements of his world were to be removed.

There is shouting. Lots of shouting. One of the council men tries to take the fishing rod, but the man who comes to fish won't let go. They struggle, then the council man stalks away, barking madly. The others jeer. The man who comes to fish darts forward and picks up the little canvas stool, peeling it from the mud like a sliver from a wound. He turns to go, and as he walks away the council men howl at him. He turns around only once, red-faced, bucket swinging loosely in his hand, but then a stone thrown by one of the yellowjackets plops down into the scum not an arm from where he stands and he startles, burrows hurriedly away into the trees.

Grundy watches all this from his place on the shore, the rock glued to his hand by its caustic coating of mud. It feels as though something has been ripped out of him, taking breath and heartbeat with it, leaving his other insides to cave slowly into the empty space like floes of melting ice. He drops the rock and sinks down to watch the council men, hating their loudness, their arrogance, their smooth shiny heads encased in armour.

A hand finds his shoulder. It's the clown - he knows without even looking. Grundy hisses silence at him. The clown is on all fours, muddier than ever, face long and scared. He points at the council men, pulls a monstrous face, points at Grundy and himself, then jerks his head towards the trees. When he goes, Grundy follows, creeping with muscle-straining care until both are out of earshot of the yellow-jacketed men.

The waste is vast, Grundy knows. Bigger than he could possibly hope to reckon, stretching through the world like a cat's leg crooked and bristling with tributaries. His part comprises the scum pond and the pylon and the fat block of land that leads down along the brook. He follows the clown this far and then stops, uncertain. The clown pays no attention, not even looking back. This reassures Grundy: he prefers it that the neither of them care.

A sharp slope plunges from the trees to the grease flats. Part scum and part mud and lacquered with oil that sits sludging and self-satisfied atop the wet. As they splash through inch-deep puddles rainbows fracture and wobble themselves into pretty shapes, then disappear. The clown's baggy silk trousers are already dried black to the knee, and soon Grundy is spattered as well.

At the far end of the grease flats the forest picks up again. They lose themselves in the thin line of trees, walking until the clown comes to an abrupt halt, gloved hand held skyward. They creep, edging, leaving a trail of oily leaves and blackened footprints. The clown points ahead, through a screen of bitter greenery.

There. Sitting in the midst of an earthen nest is a thing as yellow as the council men, but many times larger. In memory, Grundy has never seen a thing like it. It reminds him of the pylon, but squatter, more complicated, loaded with threat. No clean, high lines of metal. No reaching wires and space and firmly planted feet. Instead it sits on mud-gunked wheels, a yellow arm enfolded like a scorpion's tail, the scoop at the end worn down to silver metal teeth.

Even from the trees, Grundy can smell it. Stench as thick as rotting, but twisted over on itself, chemical in its complexity. The clown looks at him with wide eyes, a rim of white make-up still staining the lids.

Night. They sneak up on it from the trees, crawling low through the earth and dirt and expecting any moment a light or the council men or the thing itself to roar to life. The clown goes first, hauling himself up onto the wheel and flinging open the door to the cab. There's no council man inside. While the clown busies himself there Grundy circles the beast, noting the deep cuts it has made in his earth, the mud and leaves that cling to the tracks.

Thick wires curl like loops of gut from the crook of the arm. Grundy steps up onto the scoop and rips at them. Bolts pop. He loses a fingernail, sticks the injury in his mouth then pulls again. Something gives. The clown has found a rock and is smashing the controls, each impact ringing like the hum of the pylon. The wires slither out, bunched in Grundy's fist, and he pulls them till the holdings snap. He flings them down and spits.

That night Grundy sits outside his shack and chews the last of his cigarettes, the tobacco turning muddy between his teeth. At night, in the great distance, there are lights above the marsh. Steady sometimes, or else blinking like flares of gas. The lights are the world of the council, all complicated and boxy. No mud there, no scavenge, no thick water. No waking to birds, no smell nor soft moistbody warmth of shack.

Grundy was part of it once. He senses this, even when his mind is at its most senseless. It had him, and he escaped, like a bird ripping itself from the fangs of a cat, leaving behind a part that will never regrow, that the cat will eat down to bones and shit back into the earth. Grundy shakes himself, scratches his neck till it reddens, then crawls into his home to sleep.

They come for him the next day. Early morning, earlier than he's ever known the council men to be abroad. He wakes to the shack falling in with a bang and a crash. After weathering storms and floods and the onslaught of winters the whole thing doesn't stand up to more than a hammer blow, and the boards fall onto Grundy and knock his ribs in. He splutters up into pain and red breath. Hands claw through the detritus.

He explodes. Up on his feet even though his chest feels like it's gaping open. Five of them, a few with hammers or hacksaws, low on their haunches, faces bared. He spits and screams at them. When one crashes into him from behind he finds a muscled arm with his teeth and bites down until loose hot flesh falls onto his tongue.

One wails away, but more pile in. Hands seize wrists, legs. Something heavy slams into his spine and he is squashed down face first into mud, still thrashing and kicking all the while. Something hard and rounded taps his skull and the world, the scents and the stinks of it, comes unspooled. Grundy tastes fish. Something thin and leathery cinches around his wrists.

They carry him at a quick trot, face down, the ground rushing by underneath. Grundy growls and hollers and gnashes his teeth. He can't move, and it's only the very tips of their boots he can see. He would spit at them, but when he tries the spit comes out sick-like and stringy. He recognises the thick mud of the grease flats. Cold blobs of it fly up and paste themselves into his face. And then they drop him, and a steel-toed boot pins him by the chest. They are in the clearing with the machine, the ghastly yellow thing now lying in shivered pieces. Grundy feels happiness at the sight of it. Wild, roaring happiness. And then he sees the clown.

Most of the make-up from his face is gone to blood and bruising. The swollen star around his eye weeping into a slur. Slumped in the scoop of the yellow machine like a sacrifice, like one of the fish the man used to leave. Maybe dead. Grundy sees this, and sees all the council men, the army of yellow hats and jackets that fill the clearing and the happiness turns vicious and black, snapping at the bottom of his lungs. But the boot and the leg that fills it still weigh on his broken chest.

They're all waiting for something. Someone. Grundy waits too. Every time he breathes it feels as though his ribs fall a little further out of their spaces. The yellowjackets stir, and some of them part, and in the space there is a council man in a suit, a white hat, long black legs sheathed in rubber boots. There's a snug sheaf of papers beneath his arm, emblazoned with markings in black and red. Grundy feels himself go very still, every bright internal instinct freezing like a fawn. The yellowjackets don't matter anymore. The worst they could ever do was kill him.

The whitehat makes noises and the men coo and moo and circle about. Some of them have hammers, and one holds a dented red can which sloshes as though full of grease. A yellowjacket holds up Grundy's head by a handful of mud-cracked greying hair. The council man bends close enough to smell (like the yellow machine, like fat and stained knives) and pulls out a little black box. Grundy squirms, but the hand is firm and it only strains his neck. Click. A bright light from the box that pierces right the way through his skull. The whitehat makes a note on his papers. One of the yellowjackets unreels a length of metal tape.

Grundy is so absorbed in spitting and cursing the yellowjackets that he doesn't see the clown move. He's still dazed from the light, and when he hears screaming he looks up to find a yellowjacket already floundering in the mud, blood pissing through his hi-vis. The clown is free, leather ligaments still wrapped around his wrists but frayed away, grated down to thread against the sharp angles of the yellow machine. As the clown comes splashing over, arms wide, some sharp jag of metal glinting in the grip of his glove, none of the yellowjackets move. All stare in shock at their fallen man.

The whitehat yammers and windmills back. The one pinning Grundy goes too, arms up, slow to bring his hacksaw to bear. Grundy thinks that the clown might murder him first, and the savage happiness roars back... but no, he bulls through, drops to his knees and swiftly severs the ligaments that hold Grundy's hands.

Grundy springs, raging, elemental. All the yellowjackets are still stirring through the muck. He seizes the bit of shrapnel from the clown (a brief fight for it, the clown's mangled face toothy and wide) and finds it big and lumpy, trailing fittings and bits of wire. He falls on the whitehat and drives it home, into the soft bit of his face, in deep below the helmet, which tumbles off to reveal a bald and burnished scalp.

Then, as the yellowjackets start to muster, the clown and Grundy run.

Both are sprinting when they slither down into the dry bed of the creek. The clown is ahead of Grundy, blundering along kicking up dust and stones. Where the creek dries up they scramble into the woods and stop, just within the shade of trees. Grundy spits and heaves, hands on knees, shrugging. Ribs like knives now, like a rack of razors dipping in and out his lungs.

From here they can see the pylon, and the other pylons after it, descending towards the horizon, hand in hand like soldiers gradually sinking into quicksand. The wires that swoop above them buzz now, and Grundy thinks that even at night they will be able to follow the wire, its yearning growlish sound.

Distantly too he can hear the yellowjackets slobbering through the grease. There is time to catch his breath, to huff and clutch until the stabbing stitch of his lungs recedes. And then they run again, towards the next metal tower and the next and the next, leaving behind what Grundy knows, losing themselves in the endless waste.

Martin Cromie

Martin Cromie was born in 1956 and obtained a BA English from The New University of Ulster. He worked in Local Authority and Education administration for 35 years before seizing an early retirement opportunity in 2011 to begin a new career in writing. In 2012 he completed an MA in Creative Writing at the Seamus Heaney Centre, Queens University Belfast and is currently undertaking a PhD in Creative Writing. He was shortlisted for the Brian Moore Short Story Competition, longlisted for the Fish Short Memoir Competition and published in the *Nottingham Short Story Anthology 2012*. He lives in Newry, Northern Ireland.

Stop Press

1 2.58 p.m. Newland's Cross, Naas dual carriageway, County Kildare. The first shot splinters the glass. Blood oozes from her white blouse. A white motorbike hovers alongside her car. She is frozen, one hand on the steering wheel, the other clawed on the gear stick. She sees two men, black leather jackets, white helmets. Her foot loses muscle and slips the clutch. The red Opel Calibra spasms forward. The engine shuts down. Her head rolls like a rag doll. Her eyes stare through the cataract fog of dying. The pillion passenger arches towards her, black leather shrouding the June sunshine. A light halo bounces from his helmet. He squeezes the Colt Python's finger-moulded trigger. Her body sucks up .357s, absorbing the gun cracks in muffled thumps; one...two...three...four...five. Her blue eyes stare, lids quivering, signalling the death of nerves.

12.59 p.m. The bike revs tickle the passenger's thighs. He hits the bike driver's shoulder. Her dead dilated pupils catch his. He turns away. The bike springs and banks into Belgard Road. He shoves the Colt inside his jacket. Muzzle heat seeps through the layers of clothes. In front of him the driver's tensed shoulders shudder in time with his own body as the bike tyres hit pebbles and pock marks on the tarmac. The white helmet lacquer reflects a kaleidoscope of traffic mingling in the ordinariness of the afternoon.

1.00 p.m. The driver bends the bike towards Tallaght. They weave at a steady rate through a maze of cloned council estate streets. On Airton Road the singing gear changes range alto to bass and he feels the brakes gristle. The driver shunts the bike to a stop behind a blue '89 Fiesta parked in a derelict industrial site. The passenger gets off. The bike lifts and twists into dense housing. The driver doesn't look back. Inside the Fiesta the passenger takes off the jacket and helmet. The false moustache prickles as he rips it from his face. He slips out of the padded body-warmer and lumber shirt. The Colt is still warm. Everything fits in a blue Gola sports bag on the passenger side floor. The Fiesta ignition fires first time. He does a u-turn, lights a Marlboro, winds down the window and drives towards the N81.

1.25 p.m. He parks in a clear space on Ballinteer Avenue, lifts a backpack from the rear seat and leaves the keys in the car. He unchains a Raleigh 10 speed from a lamp post beside the parking space and cycles through Clonard. The thermos in his backpack jags his shoulder blade. He can smell egg and onion sandwiches.

1.35 p.m. At Sandyford Industrial Estate he leaves the bike in his usual spot in the corner of the building supply yard car park. On his way to the staff locker room he takes off the brown kid gloves and buries them in a full rubbish skip. Plenty of time before he clocks on for the two-to-ten shift.

It is the end of lunchbreak. In the 'Staff Only' area morning shift workers change out of protective clothing, ready for home. New shift arrivals gear up with steel-capped boots, hard hats, earmuffs, gloves. The nine-to-five sales and office staff, with logo blazoned shirts and blouses, sit or stand in long-forged groups, coffee mugs in hand. He goes to his locker, takes out his gear and removes the flask and sandwiches from his backpack, placing them upright, in line, on the top shelf. He sits the backpack on the locker floor, padlocks the door and clips the key to his belt.

"Some news, that, wasn't it?"

He looks to his side. Manus O'Donnell, the shift foreman, is putting his boots on. "About Veronica Guerin?" he adds.

"What news is that?" the man asks, looking at Manus.

"Shot dead, she was, just there now." Manus stops tying his laces and looks up. "It's on all the radio shows, didn't you hear?"

The man sits alongside Manus. He starts to put his own boots on. "No," he says, "I was on the bike from home. I'm just in. Never heard any news."

"They shot her out at Newlands Cross. In broad daylight." He stands, clomps his boots on the floor, making sure they're comfortable for the next eight hour's work. "Jesus. Poor girl," he says, "And her with a wee boy and all."

"That's rough," the man says. He gets up, hangs the earmuffs around his neck, puts gloves in the patch pockets of his cargo pants and pats his shirt pocket to make sure his cigarettes and lighter are there. He looks at the clock on the wall. 1.50 p.m. "Smoke before we start?"

Manus nods. They lift their hard hats and walk to the door. Outside a youth leans against a parked car. Manus and the man light up. They walk towards the car. A woman inside the car holds her hands over her cheeks. "Oh my God!" she says. The radio is turned up and the window is fully wound down. A reporter is giving a stuttering account 'live from the scene' on the Naas dual carriageway. "Well, Eoin?" asks Manus, "What's the latest?"

The youth leans his elbow on the roof of the car. He is straining to hear the radio, his head tilted towards the driver's window. "Two blokes on a bike took her out," he smiles. "Six shots…boom!" Eoin points his hand with two fingers, gun-barrel shaped, through the wound down window space. "Boom," he says.

"That's not one bit funny, you wee gobshite," the woman shouts, smacking Eoin on the hand.

Eoin laughs. "What's got you so annoyed, anyway." he says, moving away from the car towards the workshops. "Sure didn't she grass up all them boys to the cops, just to make a name for herself, the bitch." He swaggers off miming gunshots in the air. "Boom, boom," he shouts and laughs.

Manus turns towards the woman in the car. "Don't take any notice, Maureen," he says, "That Eoin fella's soft in the head. Thinks he's one of the lads, like. Hasn't the brains he was born with."

Maureen smiles. "I know that," she says, "But, I mean, for Christ's sake, you'd think even a wee thug like that would have a bit of cop-on, wouldn't you?"

The man stubs his cigarette out on the tarmac. He looks at his watch. 1.59 p.m. "I'd better get started," he says to Manus, "I've a big order to get out." He puts his hard hat on. "Sixteen roof trusses and timbers."

"I'll be there in a few minutes," Manus say. He turns and listens to the radio. The two o'clock headlines repeat the main story. The man goes to the timber shed. The mechanical saws have not yet been started up after the lunch break. Another radio is tuned in to FM 104. "Gardai are asking witnesses to come forward," the sombre announcer says.

"Some fuckin' chance!" shouts another young worker, leaning against the wall, looking around the faces of his workmates for some sort of affirmation.

The radio announcer gives staccato facts "two men….white helmets… black leather jackets…."

The man nods at the workers nearby. They nod back or wave. He lifts a clipboard off a nail, grabs a tape measure and chalk. He walks towards the stacks of honey coloured roof timbers at the end of the shed. "…a large white motorbike, Honda or Yamaha…" continues the announcer, "Registration 89 D 4823…"

He sits the clipboard on a shelf, takes a pencil from his shirt pocket and checks the work docket. "Sixteen trusses. 12 metres wide. 2.6metre pitch," he whispers, tallying the number of lengths of timber needed, and the cuts required. The man double checks his mental arithmetic. He writes out a final list then chalk marks selected timbers lying, edge out, in the bays. He marks eight with an 'X' to denote those to be cut in two then angled as uprights for the roof pitch. The rest are given a tick. He looks at his watch. 2.20 p.m. By now the bike will be at the bottom of the Grand Canal. The Fiesta will be in a lock up somewhere on the Southside.

The mechanical saws are operating. Everyone wears earmuffs and the sound of transistor radios is drowned out for a while. One final check and he walks towards two men with metal grippers. He explains the contents of the docket using a mixture of pointing, shouting and reference to the list of figures. When he is content that the men understand, he pats one of them on the shoulder and gives the thumbs up. The men start to pull the timbers out with the grippers. They load them on a forklift and drive them to the other side of the shed where the saw blades are whining at high pitch, amber dust misting the warm sunlight that spills in through the shed's hanger doors.

Manus joins him in the cutting area. They get to work on sawing the roof timbers. The noise prevents conversation. Halfway through the order Manus signals to the man, lifting an imaginary cup to his lips. The man stops the saw, covers the blade with a metal guard and walks out into the open yard. He and Manus buy coffee in the canteen. The 4.00 p.m. news on the radio echoes. Conversation volume is low. People at tables, in the queue, and behind the counter listen to the latest details. The man hears a witness describe the killer as tubby, fair skinned, about thirty years old with a moustache. Nice to have ten years shaved off, he thinks. Shame about the extra weight, though.

A reporter interviews the Minister for Justice. She says something about such killers being difficult to catch. "There is no connection between the victim and the person who carries out the murder," she emphasises. The man thanks the girl behind the counter for the coffee. He sorts through coins for the exact change and pays the cashier. "The killer is hired specifically for the purpose," the Minister concludes.

Back in the yard Manus and the man sit on a wall. They light cigarettes. "What the hell's this world coming to?" says Manus. The man looks at the ground, inhales smoke, sips coffee.

"I mean, how could anybody do that, just shoot a woman and not even think of her family?" Manus looks around the yard as if searching for an answer.

"It's a strange world alright," says the man. "Most people seem to be very upset about it, don't they?"

Manus drinks some coffee. "It's funny," he says, "but round here you have those that think Veronica Guerin's a saint because she was doing all she could to clear the streets of them dope peddlin' shites like Gilligan." He draws on his cigarette. "Then there's wee bastards like Eoin that think Gilligan and co. are gods. Bloody celebrities or something."

Manus looks sideways at the man. "You're not a Dub and you don't live in a bloody run down housing estate, so it's hard to see what I mean, you know?"

The man nods. "No offence," Manus says. He finishes his coffee.

"None taken," the man answers.

On their way back to the workshop they finish their cigarettes and stub them out before they get near to the timber piles. "So," asks Manus, "you're off for two weeks from Friday?"

"Yes," the man says. "I'll be glad of a rest."

"Going anywhere nice?"

"Day here and there. Nowhere in particular," he says.

They put earmuffs back on and start up the saw. The man checks what items remain on the job docket. He checks his watch. 4.15 p.m. The Colt would be in a smelter in a backstreet foundry near Dublin port. On Friday he will finish at 6.00 p.m. He will ride his bike to the boarding house, change, pack his one suitcase and backpack. In the taxi taking him to the airport he will find an envelope in the pouch behind the driver's seat. The envelope will contain a ticket to Chicago and a key to a downtown mail box. In it he will find twenty thousand dollars.

The saw grinds the final piece of timber for the roof job order. The man signals to Manus who nods as if to say 'good job'. He checks his watch again. 5.30 p.m. A half hour break coming up at 6.30 p.m. He feels hungry for egg and onion sandwiches.

Allan Drew

Allan Drew is a stay-at-home dad, a when-he-can writer, and an often-student. After leaving school he studied molecular biology and biochemistry. Subsequently, he spent three years in medical research and thirteen years as a writer/editor/ middle manager in a medical publishing company. Allan has since completed graduate and masters qualifications in English and Creative Writing. His poems and short stories have been published in a number of literary journals and magazines, and his short fiction has won and been short-listed/commended in several competitions. Allan is currently waiting for the southern hemisphere spring to emerge so that he can renovate his lawn.

Transit of Venus

No one in the lab knew I had once had eleven fingers. Until Heather.

Heather was a Masters student. Youngish. Thinnish. Tattoo on her inner forearm – a comet. Yellow painted fingernails. Standard issue. On her first morning I learned she hadn't used a pipette before.

"How is that possible?" I asked.

"My lab partner always did that sort of thing," she said. "I would do the write-up." She didn't seem worried.

"This is a P100," I said. She looked at it like it was from Mars.

"What does P100 stand for?" This was the first question she asked me, the first of infinity.

"It's a Gilson Pipetman, you can measure out ten to a hundred microlitres."

"Right. How does it work?" she asked. I showed her the dial and the necessary thumb action.

"Awesome. Microlitres are so small. How do they get it so accurate?"

When I showed her the P2 and pipetted one microlitre, she high-fived me.

I'd been assigned as her buddy, and I'd train her for the first two months. At the scheduled afternoon tea on her first day, I asked her about herself. She said she was recently married.

She'd asked her fiancé not to mow the lawn before their backyard wedding. "I wanted to glide to him on an aisle of daisies," she said. She drank a strong black sort of tea. I sipped my instant coffee.

"Daisies are my favourite flower," she said. "What's yours?"

"I'm not sure." Daisies were a weed. I dug them out of my lawn with an old paring knife.

"Think about it," she said.

Part of the problem was that Heather had studied physiology. She'd spent too much time with animals and organs; not enough time with DNA. She came to our lab, across the walkway and down the stairs from Physiology, for her Masters project because she wanted new experience. That, and there was a shortage of supervisors upstairs.

I'd worked with plenty of Masters students. I'd been in the lab ten years, and there was a pattern. They apply, they get accepted, they pay their fees, they get a supervisor, and that supervisor gets me to train them. It's the system. These students come and go each year, drift in and out. Some come back to do doctoral studies. When they get their Masters they become insufferable. When they get their PhDs they become incomprehensible – for a while at least, then they settle down.

I had set aside time in that first week to show her the methodologies we ran. We were at the bench.

"You ever run a Southern blot?"

"What's that?" she said. The equipment was spread out in front of us.

"It's for detecting particular sequences of DNA. You'll need to know this." Her project was on bacterial genes responsible for antibiotic resistance. "You separate out all the lengths of DNA, and use a radiolabelled probe to find the bit you're interested in." I showed her the tray we used for the procedure, about the size of a lunchbox.

"What's so Southern about it?"

"It was named after Edwin Southern," I said.

"Oh. I thought the direction was important."

"What?" I said. She placed an empty beaker upside down on her palm.

"You said radiolabelled. Like radioactive?" she asked.

"Yes, 32P."

"32P?"

"The radioactive isotope. Phosphorous 32. You come across it before?"

"Not that I know of." She shrugged, and rolled the gel tray over like she was inspecting it for defects.

"You have to be careful. 32P undergoes beta decay, moderately active." I tried to think of a better way to explain it. "It can cause radiation damage. It's mutagenic."

"What?" She looked up and squinted at me.

"It releases a high energy electron, during decay."

"Electron? Why is everything so small?" She reached for a pipette and practised the action.

"Hang on. What?" I said. "Not everything is small."

"Everything around here is," she said. I was getting distracted.

"Look, you need perspex at least a centimetre thick between it and you, at all times. You ever use a Geiger counter?" I pointed to a machine like an old-fashioned phone. She shook her head.

"You turn it on like this."

The Masters students get a shared office, and I went there to find her. She was late for our meeting at the autoclave. She needed to learn how to sterilise her equipment.

"Heather?" She didn't look up. She was wearing a black singlet with straps that crossed over at the back. She had a tattoo on her shoulder, sets of broken lines – like morse code – that tapered out as they crept down her arm. Her ponytail was lopsided. She was watching the screen, furiously typing into an Excel sheet. Her right hand was a blur on the number pad.

"S'up?" she said, without breaking her rhythm or turning her head.

"What are you doing?" I asked.

"Analysing the data from the other day."

"In Excel?"

"I'm working out the stats." I bent down to take a look, then pulled a chair over.

"We usually use–," and then I forgot the name of the stats program. "What's that column?"

"Standard deviation." As she plugged in the data, the standard deviations calculated themselves.

"We normally use standard error of the mean, for measures repeated in quadruplicate."

"Oh," she said. She stopped typing and inserted a new column into the sheet, labeled it "SEM."

"The mode is sometimes interesting, if you round the results," I said. She pointed to another column of the sheet, labeled "Mode" in bold font. When Heather pointed, she used her little finger. I hadn't seen anyone do that before. Her little finger was thin, white and smooth, like the bone that sat beneath the skin.

I had given my extra finger a gender and a name, when I was a kid. I called him Eleven. Only to myself. No one else really talked about him. Not even the other kids at school. They made fun of my haircut, my skin, my nose, my grades, my shoes and, later, my virginity and my car, but they never had much to say about Eleven. Perhaps, without a precedent to guide them, they didn't know how to go about it.

Eleven hung off the thumb of my right hand, had a knuckle but no nail. Although I could move him a little, he was never what you might call useful. He would catch on things, like the neck hole of my t-shirt as I pulled it over my head and the edge of the cupboard as I reached for a cup.

When I learned to write, Eleven didn't get in the way – but I said he did. I wished hard, when I was still young and thought wishes might come true, that I would become left-handed overnight, so my teacher wouldn't accidentally touch him when she corrected my grip on the pencil.

"This is the autoclave," I said.

"Autoclave," she said, and ran a finger along the edge of its steel casing.

"It's a big pressure cooker, really. You put your stuff in here," I opened the door, like a submarine's hatch, "then close it carefully. You tighten the pins—"

"I've been reading up on Southern blotting," she said.

"Really?" I said, and opened the autoclave's door and sprayed it with ethanol. "And?"

"Why don't we use a fluorescent label, rather than 32P?"

"It doesn't work as well."

"They say it does," she said.

"That's just marketing."

"Are you sure?" she asked. She wasn't the first student to get jittery about radioactive labelling. One kid almost shit himself when he first heard the Geiger counter crackle and hiss.

"The radiolabel works better," I said, "easier to quantify." I was wiping up the ethanol with a paper towel when she punched me hard on the shoulder.

"Where's your scientific curiosity?" she demanded.

As a kid I would hide Eleven – in my pocket, usually. All those protests I made against a pair of shorts or trousers were because they didn't have a pocket in which to hide him. I never told my mother, but she could have bought me pants any colour or length or style she'd wanted and I would've worn them, as long as they'd had a pocket on the right hip.

Computers became a problem. Keyboards are built for ten fingers, not eleven. Typing up my homework for school and my assignments for university was always trickier than it should've been. You might have thought that eleven fingers would be an advantage for keyboarding. They aren't. Having three legs wouldn't help in soccer, and having an extra eyebrow wouldn't make you a better frowner. In the end, anything beyond normal just gets in the way.

Heather came to work with a present for me. It was wrapped in recycled corrugated cardboard.

"But, what–" I began.

"Stop it," she said, "open it."

It contained two cupcakes that she had, quite clearly, decorated herself. On one she had written, in wobbly icing, Southern, and on the other, Blot. "Edible pets," she said. I let out a short laugh, like an exhalation.

"Not sure I want to eat a Southern blot."

"Come on, science man," she said, and she picked up Blot and ate it.

Once, in a bout of teenage mania, I went to the emergency room and demanded they cut Eleven off. I would have let them do it with an axe, at the time.

They refused. They said I would need to go through the proper channels. In the end they asked me to leave, said I was being a nuisance.

When I started university I got a job and a student loan to pay for my fees and rent, and there was enough left over to pay a surgeon. An outpatient procedure. Simple. The surgeon offered to put Eleven in a jar for me, after he'd been removed. I told him no. I guess Eleven was incinerated in some bio-waste furnace. I guess Eleven turned to smoke and ash and floated out to sea.

A few weeks in, I had lunch with Heather in the staff room.

"You're quite young to be married," I said. She looked at the ring on her finger, a large red stone on a silver band.

"I love him," she said. She took a meat pie out of a brown paper bag and started eating.

"Of course. But still, it's quite young."

"What do you mean?"

"Don't most people have a long engagement, or live together first?"

"We wanted to get started."

"Fair enough," I said. She put her pie down and looked out the window. The profile of her nose was a perfect triangle.

"What's your husband's name?"

"Mike," she said, and for some reason I was disappointed.

"Would you like a bite?" She held up her half-eaten pie, exposing its open insides to me with a questioning look on her face.

I held up my sandwich. "I'm all sorted," I said.

Heather looked out the window again. "Cloudy."

"Yeah," I said, looking at my lunch. The cheese was cracked at the edges – over-exposure to refrigerated air.

"No chance then, I guess," she said.

I looked up. "Huh?"

"The transit of Venus. It starts soon."

"What? Really?"

"What do you mean, 'Really'? How could you not know?" she asked.

I shrugged. "This is the first chance for anyone alive today to see it – the last one seen in this hemisphere was like a hundred and twenty years ago."

"What does it look like?" I asked.

"A dark dot on the sun."

"That's all?"

"'That's all'? Oh, come on, mister. Can't you imagine it, out there, the huge void, our planets getting organized into line with the sun, lurching from their scattered orbits into a temporary order. All those millions and millions of miles, all that warped space-time? Your eyes, my eyes, seeing something like that?"

"Except it's cloudy," I scoffed. "Couldn't you see that coming?" Heather looked away, and quite suddenly my face went hot. What was it? Embarrassment? Was I repulsed by my own cynicism? Did I consider myself above galactic rarities – was celestial magnificence too mundane for my attention? I felt tiny and ugly. I put my sandwich down, unfinished. Heather stood up.

"You know what the solar system says to you?" she asked. She didn't give me the chance to reply – not that I would have taken it. She pointed out the window, and as she did so, the sky turned bright white and a yellow rectangle of winter sun struck the side of the fridge, the angle perfect for revealing the pitting and scarring in the aged enamel.

"It says 'Up yours'," she said, and she left.

I tipped the rest of my lunch in the bin. I stood at the window, leaning on the sill and wondering how I might look at the sun without being blinded. A couple of minutes later, I saw Heather exit the main doors of the building, her skirt billowing in the southerly breeze. I watched her sail across the courtyard, cross Park Road, and then skip into the Domain and disappear from view.

I didn't tell my parents I was going to have Eleven removed. I went over for dinner about a week after the operation.

"What happened?" Mum said. My hand was still bandaged.

"I had to get it removed."

"Why?"

"I broke it. The doctor said he could fix it but it would never be right, or he could amputate." I had worked out that story ahead of time.

"Amputate? How did you break it?"

"It got jammed in the door of the bus." Lots of things get jammed in the doors of buses. Why not an eleventh finger?

"Oh God. Can I see?"

"I can't take the bandage off yet."

"Does it hurt?" she asked.

"It did, but not anymore."

My two months with Heather had passed. She knew all the techniques. We were having morning tea together in the staff room, a kind of see you later, best-of-luck. Soon enough she'd be writing up, and then she'd be gone. Heather had that tea of hers, and I had an instant.

"Watch this," she said, and then she opened her mouth and turned her tongue upside down. I hadn't seen that done before. Her tongue looked alive, like some sort of blind animal that lives in a cave and tunnels about looking for other blind animals to eat. She wore dark red lipstick, and after she'd turned her tongue over, her lips glistened.

"Good grief," I said.

"What can you do?" she asked.

I had an urge to be strange, just for a minute. So I told her about Eleven.

"Eleven fingers? That's quite sinister, mister."

"Not really," I said.

"You must have copped hell at school."

"Who didn't?" I said. She pulled my hand over and held it, firmly. Her nails were painted deep blue, and on each one she had stencilled a tiny orange sun. She inspected the scar on my thumb, ran the tip of her finger along the pale white line, resting for a moment at the point of incision. It doesn't take much, sometimes, just the sensation of skin on skin, to spark the chain reaction. A tingling, or a sort of buzz – an interior vibration, like when you press your forehead to the window in a moving car: unsettling, disorientating, compelling. Or, perhaps, it was more like a sting – I felt water pooling behind my eyes, felt it asking for permission to flow. But then again, it was nothing, nothing more than the movement of ions – of charged particles – through neuronal channels, a surge of private electricity, invisible, silent, transient. She let go of my hand and opened the newspaper. I breathed.

"How's Mike?" I asked.

"Good. He's away at the moment, for work," she said. "So, what happened to this abnormality of yours?" she asked. She didn't look up from the paper but she wore a sideways smile.

I looked at my hand and the thin scalpel-line, and wondered if Eleven would want me to obscure the truth. "It got caught in the door of a bus."

"No shit?" she said.

"Yeah."

"Do you miss it?" She turned a page of the newspaper.

"What do you mean?" I hadn't thought about it like that.

"Do you wish you had it now?" she said.

"I don't know. I hated it, back then."

"Why?"

I had to think, to remember why, exactly. "It kept getting in the way."

"Of what?" she asked, and I wasn't sure what to say.

"All sorts, everything," I said. I got up and walked over to the sink. I poured the rest of my coffee down the drain and washed my mug, scalding my hands on the overheated water. I looked back to Heather, reading her paper. A ribbon of hair had come loose from her orange clip and hung over her forehead. "What're you reading about?" I asked.

She said some guy had been arrested for sitting outside a shop and intimidating people by being too still and refusing to do anything at all. She showed me the article.

"It's hard to know what to make of it," I said.

"They should have let him be."

"You think?" I said. She folded the newspaper and slapped it down on the table.

"It would have been more interesting. You arrest him, you know how it turns out. You leave him to it, it's more exciting. It's unknown."

"I guess." I said.

She looked at me. "Don't guess," she said, and handed me the paper. "Got to go now." I watched her slip her arms through the sleeves of her lab coat.

"How's the fluorescent probe working out?" I asked.

"Still fiddling with the method. Making progress though." She fastened one button on her coat, at her navel. "Thanks," she said.

"I'll see you around, then," I said.

"Of course you will." She walked off down the corridor, re-fixing the clip in her hair, and disappeared around the corner.

Uschi Gatward

Uschi Gatward was born in East London and lives there now. She read English at King's College, Cambridge and completed an MA in Creative Writing at the University of Sussex. *Pink Lemonade* is her first publication.

Pink Lemonade

Cursing Jessica and Miroslawa, I pelt along the Commercial Road with my daughter in the sling, knees groaning at every jolt. At the crossing for the station we meet another mum, with a two-year-old in a buggy. I recognize the look of agitation more than the face, but I've seen her somewhere before.

"Just in time," I say.

She nods. "These lights are always slow."

We make it to the island and then to the other side, articulated lorries menacing us with their engines.

We get to the station at ten on the dot. Jessica and Miroslawa, in cagoules, stand at the centre of a small group.

Miroslawa is looking faintly embarrassed, as well she might, and is holding a large white cardboard box, which is already lightly drizzle-spattered. Jessica clutches a clipboard and guards an enormous plastic crate by the station entrance. I know some of the other families: Sushmila and her mum, and a white couple I've met in the park with their newborn.

"Goo-oood morning," says Miroslawa, with that slightly twinkly, slightly world-weary way she has, that says *'I have seen worse hardship than this.'*

I take Jessica's clipboard, hold it at arm's length past my sling, run my finger down to find our names, tick the box to say I've paid, and sign the disclaimer.

"Does that cover land-based drowning?" I quip.

Jessica opens her crate. "I've brought wellies," she says. "And waterproofs for everyone. What's Katie's size?"

"A five or six should do it."

She hands me the wellies and a red all-in-one hooded waterproof, '18-24' emblazoned on the front in marker pen, with the Centre's initials.

I nod at Miroslawa's box.

"Cakes," she says with a quiet lift of her eyebrows. "It's Ayo's birthday."

"O-o-ohhhh." I raise my head in greeting to Ayo's parents, both of them here today, standing slightly apart, smart in belted jeans and ironed shirts. They smile. His mum's got an oxygen canister on her back, attached by a long plastic tube to Ayo's nose, and his father pushes a holiday-sized suitcase. I smile at them and keep smiling as I let my gaze fall away.

"His first trip to the sea," murmurs Miroslawa.

"Here are your train tickets," says Jessica. "And this is just a little activity pack."

The Ziploc bag contains a small satsuma, three cheap crayons, a sheet of paper and a green sand mould in the shape of a starfish. She'll like that.

Nancy, my Chinese friend, arrives, bumping her buggy up the stairs. She's not normally late.

I go to help her. "You thought it would be cancelled?"

She laughs. "I waited for a text. It's gonna piss with rain."

"Never mind, I've got Factor 50 sunscreen in my bag. They can share it."

Nancy signs the clipboard, pays the balance, and gets waterproofs, wellies and a blue seahorse for Ava.

She shows it to me. "It's nice of them, right? They don't have to do this."

"Yeah. It is."

Miroslawa comes over to us. "We're still waiting for six families. But we don't want to miss the best of the day …"

Nancy and I swap looks.

"… So we'll get on the train in one group now, and Jessica will wait for the others."

"Righty-o." I adjust my sling, and heave my bag onto my shoulder.

"Can I carry something?" says Miroslawa. It's the guilt.

"I'm all right," I say. "You look after those cakes."

"Cakes?" says Nancy.

"It's little Ayo's birthday. The twenty-four weeker."

"O-o-ohhhhh." She turns to stare at them. "Is that oxygen?"

"Must be." I don't look round, and try to push ahead a bit so they don't hear us. But when we're all on the platform I stroll over and crouch down by the buggy to say happy birthday. I don't take his hand because I don't know where he is with infection control, although I presume he's all right if he's allowed on an outing.

As the train approaches, Miroslawa shouts out that we'll all get in the last carriage. It's almost empty anyway. No one with any sense is going to the seaside, not today.

Nancy and I find two four-seats across the aisle from each other so we can spread out. I tip Katie out of the sling and set her up at the tiny side-table with the crayons while I peel the satsuma and rummage in my bag for a bib to save her t-shirt.

Miroslawa perches opposite me to take a photo of Katie and then one of Ava, also drawing, with the view behind her.

"I think we're going to be lucky with the weather," she smiles.

As if in answer, a sound like gravel spatters the window next to me and runs down the glass.

I get out my ticket in case the inspector comes by, and stare at it, calculating how many bus rides to the city farm we could get for the price.

Nancy passes me popcorn and I pass her rice cakes, spreading them with

Philadelphia from a plastic knife.

"Look, Katie!" I say, as fields enter my sightline. "Sheep!" I reach over and lift her up to the window. "We might even see some horses!" And we do, whole herds of them.

As the sky clears a bit and the rain dries up, the landscape changes to a silty grey, lined with tall chimneys and shipping containers: industrial Essex. We pass Pitsea and I kneel up on the seat for the first glimpse. I see Nancy slip Katie a biscuit while I'm not looking, huge diamond on her finger dazzling me as usual.

Then I spot it, in the distance. "Katie, there it is!" I say. "The sea! It's the sea!"

Miroslawa comes back down the carriage and leans on the headrests repeating the same phrase. "Just two more stops, so if you want to use the toilets, change nappies …"

We're coming into Leigh-on-Sea now. Weekends in my grandmother's caravan – but I haven't been here in years. I start humming an old TV ad jingle, to the tune of Dylan's 'Subterranean Homesick Blues' (though I found that out later): "Ma in Marlow, JEAN IN HARLOW! Lee in Leigh-on-Sea, all saving merrily." I watched that on my grandma's telly too, great big rented beast.

"Next stop," says Nancy as we pass Leigh Marina, and I start gathering the things back into my bag. The window's filled with nothing but grey sea now: sea, and the occasional derelict warehouse. Boats in rows, hundreds of them, keels upward or tarpaulined over, lying yards from the track; an old seaside shelter, empty. I sweep a wet wipe over the table as a gesture at the crayon marks and scoop up the crumbs and the peel. I put it in Nancy's outstretched hand and she pops it in the bin. I slip on my sling, chuck Katie over my shoulder and wrestle her fat legs into it. "Here we are," yodels Miroslawa down the carriage. Nancy stuffs Ava back into her buggy and we all pile off the train.

The station is an old-fashioned coastal one, whitewash and iron girders painted battleship grey.

"You can see the beach from here," says Miroslawa. "And it's not too cold!"

There's no lift, so we help with the buggies.

At the exit we turn right and file down a zigzag ramp to the beach – a long, thin, shingled stretch of shoreline punctuated by wooden breakers. There's nothing here – no tourism. Across the estuary from us, a power plant and a row of gas holders.

We pass a two-by-two crocodile of orange-tabarded three-year-olds, also out on their end of year treat. They each carry a bucket and spade.

"There's a shelter a bit further along," says Miroslawa, "and some toilets. We'll camp ourselves near there. There's a drinks shack too, nearby, so we'll have everything we need."

The shelter is round the back of the toilet block and itself looks like the proverbial brick privy, rotting benches running round inside in a horseshoe shape.

"We can leave the bags here," she says. "There's no one else around."

We dress the babies in the waterproofs and wellies. With her hood up, Katie looks like a small spaceman. Nancy and I and Sushmila's mum lead our daughters up the ramp to the beach.

I shuffle off my plimsolls and peel back my jeans to mid-calf. It's like walking across a bed of nails, but the tide's in, so there's not far to go. I test one foot in the water: freezing. Katie waddles in with her wellies, eyes shining.

"Not too deep, now. It'll get into your boots."

"Toes!" says Katie.

"Really?" I take off her wellies and socks and roll up her leggings and waterproofs, wincing as she places her feet on the stones.

Sushmila's mum slips off her sandals and wades straight in, in her salwar kameez, sopping wet cloth clinging to her legs.

Miroslawa approaches, smiling, and takes a picture. "This part is a natural pool," she says, tracing a rectangle marked out by poles. "When the tide goes out it stays full of water. It really sparkles in the sunlight. Normally it's full of kids. Full of water wings and lilos." She sighs. "This area is always busy. You have to come early to get a good spot."

We turn towards some noise and see Jessica and the latecomers, crunching down the beach towards us. The Chinese woman from Monday Rhyme Time and two families I haven't seen before.

"It's nearly twelve o'clock," calls Jessica. "I think we should eat our packed lunches before it rains."

Miroslawa nods and goes to help her with the picnic blanket. As they spread it, it whips up above their heads like a parachute. Jessica weights down one corner with stones but the wind blows them back in her face. Eventually they get all the corners and the middle ballasted with bags. Just then the first drops of rain start to fall, big and splashy. Katie and I stay put. The water's icy on my ankle bones. Ayo's mum determinedly paces the beach, oxygen bottle on her back, following Ayo as he crawls in front of her on the leash of his tube, trying to put stones in his mouth. The babies in their hooded waterproofs and wellies stagger over the shingle picking at seaweed, like so many tiny hazardous waste operatives. As the rain gets steadier, Jessica and Miroslawa pull up the blanket and pack up, gesturing that they're going to the shelter.

The Rhyme Time woman speaks in Mandarin and Nancy laughs as she replies, then turns to me.

"I think we're gonna head into the town and get chips there. You coming?"

I shake my head. "Don't think so. We've got our lunch."

As the rain starts to power down on us we all struggle back into our shoes. Sushmila's mum wrings out her trousers. From further up the beach we see all the nursery children in their little tabards and shorts, rushing along with their buckets and spades and fishing nets on sticks, herded by bad-tempered teaching assistants. Our group's staked out the shelter, so I don't know where they'll go.

Some of the families have already found the drinks shack. The white woman I know from the park sits ensconced on the bench, hands wrapped round a hot coffee. Bet she'd like a fag to go with it but she won't light up in front of Miroslawa. I grimace in sympathy.

The air is damp in the shelter. The bench is slightly damp too, so I spread out my sling to sit on. Soon we're all crowded in. The Chinese contingent has sloped off to find town, chips and tea, steaming up the hill with their buggies, raincovers on.

I unwrap our sandwiches from the clingfilm and pass one to Katie, wiping her hands as I do. Wish I'd brought a flask, I could murder a cup of tea.

The shelter is stuffed now, with people and prams, and their breath. Not everyone's got a seat, so they're just standing in the middle and the rain isn't letting up. One of the standing women pulls out a train timetable and her friend gets her things together.

As Katie and I crunch cucumber slices, Jessica moves through the shelter murmuring rumours of cake. She wades through the bags and buggies and makes her way to Ayo's family, who are sitting near me.

"Shall we do the cake now?" she says.

Ayo's father takes the white box off his lap and sets it down on the flat of the suitcase in front of him, like a coffee table. Ayo's mother holds him on her knees.

Jessica drags the coffee table out a little, to give it some room, then she stands on tiptoes and cups her mouth in her hands.

"We're doing cake now," she calls out to everyone, swaying from side to side. She taps the shoulders of the people around her and gestures to the box, making a space around it. We all do the same, signalling and shushing each other in a ripple outwards. She brings the people in from outside the shelter.

Ayo's father opens the lid of the box and I gasp. Instead of doughnuts and pastries from the bakery, there is one huge square cake. I recognize the style – it's from the shop on the lane that makes them to order, and I realize it's not from Jessica and Miroslawa but from Ayo's parents. The edges are piped in blue and the decoration is a cartoon tiger striped in black and orange. The words say 'Happy 2nd Birthday Ayomide.' The whole cake is banded with thick blue shiny ribbon in an enormous bow.

Jessica opens a carrier bag and passes out a knife, napkins and two candles in holders. Ayo's father pushes the candles into the soft icing.

"Let's sing 'Happy Birthday'," says Jessica.

"Oh, let's light the candles," I say. "Someone'll have some matches …" I trail off, realizing no one will admit to it.

"The oxygen," says Ayo's mum.

I blush and step back into the crowd.

We sing 'Happy Birthday' and then Ayo's father picks up the cake with the candles that can't be lit, and takes it round the shelter, picking his way over bags to show it to people who couldn't see.

Then he kneels down and unzips the suitcase and lets its lid fall back. It's full of party stuff: pink, blue, yellow, silver, gold and a foam of tissuey streamers. He pulls out handfuls of glossy party bags and starts handing them round, and packets of balloons, and gold paper crowns. Across the circle, Miroslawa catches my eye and then begins to blow up a red balloon

– three long puffs – ties it efficiently, hands it to a child, and takes another, stretching it between her fingers. I take a balloon and start blowing.

Ayo's father gives me a pink party bag, and a gold crown for Katie and one for me. We put them on. He takes out patterned paper plates and clear plastic cups.

Jessica brings back the cake and crouches down with it. A shame to cut it so soon, I think. Miroslawa gets out her camera. Ayo's father and mother hesitate, but they take the knife in their two hands and put Ayo's hand over it too and smile for the photo as they push it down. Jessica tries to take the cake away but Ayo's mother holds onto it.

Ayo's father goes to the suitcase again and pulls out something else. I realize then that I'd heard them clink in the case and thought they were oxygen bottles.

He unscrews the caps, tearing the paper seals, pours drinks and passes them round. Pink lemonade, the fancy kind, in glass bottles like wine, with handwritten labels with raggedy edges, the kind made with real lemons, nobody buys it unless it's on offer.

Sipping it, I see the day they imagined for their child's first birthday party. Hot, July. A day like we had for ours. All the relations turned out, neighbours popping in, cake in the garden, rugs spread out, something fizzy chilling in a bucket. Everyone saying how well she looked, how she'd lost the baby weight. Cottony seed pods and sycamore drifting down on the breeze, the baby beautiful in a party gown. I taste champagne.

Except his birthday should have been November. Cold, blustery. Maybe a day like today. And of course she never had any baby weight, never had time. Ayo's mother sits with the cake on her knees, her arms linked round it.

I look in our party bag: a packet of biscuits, lollies, felt tips, holographic stickers, a balloon – I'll save that one for later. I look around me for more balloons and the hut is filling up with them, in children's hands and bobbing along on the floor. I pick one up for Katie, a yellow one. The rain's eased to a spit, so we go outside and play on the concreted area in front of the shelter. The balloon gets whisked under a hedge, so I rescue it. Katie bats it and kicks it in front of her. An older boy, maybe two and a half, tries to join in. Katie picks up the balloon and stalks off with it, clutching it to her chest.

Jessica is finally cutting the cake, scoring it into equal rectangles, leaving a quarter of it intact for the family to take home. The unlit candles lie by its side in their holders. I've kept the wax stubs of Katie's, white for the first one and yellow for the second, in separate pouches in the cutlery drawer.

Someone passes me a napkin-wrapped slice, and I taste it. Like wedding cake: that very thick icing, the firm, slightly stale sponge and the sweetened cream.

I see Ayo's father standing next to me.

"Thank you," I say.

"It's for him," he says.

I look at Ayo and he's smiling, the surgical tape wrinkling round his cheek. I think of Katie's presents at her first birthday party and I wish I had something to give him. We didn't buy any toys for a year.

I remember the starfish. I haven't shown it to Katie yet. She's still occupied with her balloon. I pull out the bag and unzip it.

I kneel down in front of Ayo and hold it out to him. He grabs it in a chubby fist.

"Dar," he says, making the sign for 'Twinkle, Twinkle.' "Dar."

"I'm glad you like it, Ayo," I say, and squeeze his hand.

Around me, people are doing up their coats and opening umbrellas.

"I think that's it for the good weather," says Miroslawa, turning down the corners of her mouth.

The woman next to me kicks the brake off her buggy and wheels it out of the shelter. I gather up our rubbish and put away our party bag and crowns. As people start to leave, Jessica darts through the shelter with a black binliner, picking up napkins and bottles and squashed plastic cups.

Ayo's father wraps up the remaining cake and packs it carefully into the suitcase. He tries to give away some of the leftover party bags.

Miroslawa looks at her timetable. "Eight minutes to catch the next train," she says.

Katie and I start to move. She's still clutching her balloon; the raindrops drum on it. I hang back and let her toddle but she's dawdling, and the others are far ahead of us, tearing up the zigzag slope to the station. They look like people on a helter-skelter. I pick her up and put her in the sling. As we pass a side path, the wind whips up her balloon and snatches it from her hands and she howls. I run down the path after it, chasing it as it bobs away from us before being whipped up into the air again and onto some gorse where it bursts instantly, the yellow rubber caught and flapping on the thorns. Katie's face erupts in red and she screams, as if she's going to burst too.

"Never mind, Katie," I say. "We've got another one. We can blow it up on the train."

I break into a jog as we reach the zigzag, Katie bawling and arching her back all the way. Jessica trots up behind to overtake us, and Ayo's parents are a little way behind her, running with the suitcase and buggy.

"Her balloon popped," I say to Jessica as she passes us.

Jessica makes a face of concern. "I think I've got another one," she says, feeling in her bag as she runs. "I'll look on the train. And they'll have some more." She points down to Ayo's family.

"We've got one," I call after her. "Katie, you can have a red one. We'll do it on the train."

"Don't. Want. A red one," screams Katie, and she cries as if her heart is broken.

I run halfway up the zigzag, ruining my knees – we weigh what we did when I was nine months pregnant – and then I feel Katie's foot digging into me and realize she hasn't got her wellies on. I call to Jessica up ahead and run back to look for them.

"It doesn't matter," shouts Jessica, but it does. I skitter past Ayo's family to the bottom of the slope. Nothing there.

"Want the yellow one," sobs Katie. "Want the yellow one," and I hold her to me tight.

Jessica looks down at me from the top and I wave her on. As I stop and lean forward to rest I see the others running out of sight into the station and then I see the train pulling into the platform, and then out again as I lean against the zigzag wall for breath.

We watch all the carriages with the people inside chug out west round the coast towards London, carrying everyone home. Katie likes trains.

Arms around her, I walk back along the shoreline towards the brick hut. I can't see anything on the beach, but I'd like to go back to the shelter, to check. The tide's going out now, exposing mudflats. There's the pool Miroslawa talked about, peeling itself away from the sea.

Jane Healey

Jane Healey writes fiction and poetry. She has a B.A. in English Literature from the University of Warwick, an MSc in Literature & Modernity from Edinburgh University and is currently studying at Brooklyn College for an MFA in Creative Writing. She has short stories published or forthcoming in *Tin House Online*, *The Normal School* and *Fuselit*, and is currently working on her first novel. She can be found here: http://jane-healey.com

Pool Boy

She arrives home just when he pulls himself out of the pool, three piece suit clinging to his form and hair like seaweed in his eyes. His muscles strain against the sodden fabric. She thought she'd gotten rid of him already. She scowls through the kitchen window, eats the double chocolate muffin she had been saving for tomorrow and shifts her gaze so that his head is perfectly haloed by a smudgy fingerprint on the glass. He stares at her mournfully.

It's the beginning of the summer and there's a heatwave in the South East. The BBC has been showing pictures of sunbathing businesswomen in Hyde Park; Brighton beach filled with varying shades of red and pink. She had to stay late at work because people had called in sick to drive the twenty minutes to the coast.

The swimming pool is only slightly green at the edges and the water does look inviting on a hot afternoon. But she's never been a big swimmer and prefers sitting by the side and hearing water lap like kitten tongues, watching the back of the house shimmer with a watery reflection. She hasn't used the pool for a couple of years but she can still remember how the water might feel on her skin, the rough mosaiced floor on the soles of her feet.

He has been the only visitor to its chlorine depths lately and it's his hair that clogs up the filtration system. She has to pay extra to the gardener to get it cleaned. She resents this.

"I'm sorry," he says and she can hear his voice as if he was inside next to her. She hates the way he does that. She turns to the opaque Tupperware with muffin shadows in it and worries her lip with her front teeth. Maybe just one more. It's warm anyway so they'll probably go off faster. She's just being sensible.

She breaks the second muffin in two and leaves a half with the others. She'll eat it in a minute, sure, but it's worth the subterfuge. The chocolate chips melt on her swollen fingers as she glances out again and moves so that a seagull shit is perfectly placed above his head. He shakes his head like a dog and the suit makes wet slapping sounds around his torso. His tie is still on, tight at the neck.

At least it's not one of the suits she bought him, the fine grey linens from Italy. They're still in the wardrobe upstairs in their dry cleaning bags. It's one that he chose himself. She can tell by the way each small innocuous detail adds up to something vulgar – the slightly too wide lapel, the buttons that shine too much in the afternoon sun and the tie that is made of too cheap material. As she brushes the crumbs from her lips she tries to dampen down the impulse to go outside and button his waistcoat correctly. The lopsided button arrangement makes the back of her eyes itch. He always seemed to find the process of dressing challenging.

Her stomach grumbles. He has started to pace slowly along the paving stones surrounding the pool, leaving wet sloppy footprints that pale as the sun warms them. His lips are moving but she can't tell what he's saying. Probably another apology. He pauses and turns towards her.

"Please?" he says and there's almost something angry about the shape of his eyebrows so she answers before she can think,

"Please what?"

His face lights up and he starts moving towards the small lawn in front of the house. "Don't come any closer," she says. He stops at the edge of the pavement and places his pale hands in his jacket pocket. She decides then to ignore him for a bit. She's a little bit annoyed at herself for the small curls of fear that grew in her gut when he had moved towards her. Even though she knows he can't get in, not now.

She moves into the hall and up the stairs, holding onto the banister firmly and stepping through streams of sun dust. She wobbles slightly on the last step and curses under her breath. Opening the door to the bedroom, she sees her reflection frowning in the full mirror opposite. She looks fat. *Pregnant*, her best friend Sue scolded her the last time they met for lunch at the leisure centre above the sound of screaming children in the pool, *Pregnant, not fat.*

I'm eating for two, she had said to the supermarket checkout girl when she had paused pointedly while packing six packets of cake mix into a bag. If she turns to the side she'll see her shape looking alien and horrifying so she faces the mirror head-on and then neatly sidesteps towards the bed. She sinks down on top of the duvet cover, lies back and closes her eyes.

She can still feel the blue of the cotton though. *The wrong kind of blue,* she reminds herself. He had only laughed when he came home to her bedding-scorn. *There's no such thing as the wrong shade of blue,* he said and kissed her indulgently. Why was it an indulgent thing to mock her? And there was a wrong shade of blue. She was lying on it now. She'd buy another cover but they're expensive and heavy for her to carry in her condition.

She tries to sleep but it's too warm for a nap and she can sense his presence there in front of the house, almost imagine she can hear each drop of water from his suit and feel the slide of it down her own face. She brushes her forehead with a clammy hand. The baby has made her fingers swell up and lose her ankles inside prisons of fat. She has to wear slippers now, like an old lady, like her Nan.

Her Nan had called the swimming pool an outrageous extravagance when she first visited the house. *You'll only use it for a week in the summer. I just can't imagine the upkeep cost.* But her Nan thought that paper napkins were an extravagance. She missed her. Her grey hair which wouldn't ruffle in the strongest of winds, the homemade shortbread she'd bring round and the way she squeezed her hands firmly when she said goodbye. She missed that kind of certain, firm touch.

He had a weak handshake and a moist palm. It was the first thing her grandpa had said about him when he was out of the room fetching the wine glasses. A part of her was pleased that he didn't fit into what was expected of a man. That he had the muscles of a rugby player but the temperament of a poet. A regular bleeding heart. He cried at adverts for cancer charities and always let Jehovah's witnesses in for tea even if he was busy with work. And the way he dived. She scrunches up her face as if she could block the image of his graceful plunge into the water, at the bend and flex of his full calves and his cupped hands which met the surface with barely a splash at all. She's never learnt to dive and she doesn't think she ever will.

There's a noise from outside, a muffled splash, and she sits up as fast as she can with another person sloshing inside of her. Maybe he's gone. She stands and moves to the window, opening the curtains quickly so the thick embroidered fabric doesn't chafe the tight skin on her hands. She stares down at the lawn and the pool beyond it. He hasn't gone but he has thrown his suit jacket in the pool so that it floats like a jellyfish and is staring up at her window unflinchingly.

"Stop being creepy," she shouts.

He shrugs his shoulders and mouths *sorry*.

"Can't you just leave me alone?" she asks, feeling the blood beat too slowly around and around her anklebones. Her hair is stuck to the back of her neck. She hasn't been able to dye her roots; chemicals are bad for the child. "You're tiring me out," she shouts.

"Sorry!" he says. But he doesn't sound sorry. His arms look slightly thinner perhaps and his shirtsleeves are no longer dazzling white. The misbuttoning of his waistcoat is even more obvious without the jacket to shield it.

"You've buttoned up your waistcoat wrong," she says quietly. But he still hears her and looks down at the buttons, his chin creasing into his neck. He looks back up at her and smiles, shrugs his large shoulders.

"Don't you care?" she shouts, even though she doesn't have to.

"No!"

"That's not something to be proud of."

She pulls the curtains shut and breathes deeply, trying to reduce her heart rate. The doctor says it isn't good for her to get stressed, that the baby will get distressed. *Isn't that a good thing?* She had replied, *that it's de-stressed.* She had laughed and the doctor had looked at her as if she had said something very wrong. He had paused when she left the room like he wanted to ask her something more. But she just smiled wearily at him. Some people just don't enjoy jokes. The other pregnant ladies in the waiting room – Mary, Sarah and Polly among them – had given her pitying looks as she left. She knew her slippers were ugly but there was no need to pity her for them. Pregnancy had made Sarah's eyes disappear into her cheeks like a mole. If anyone should be pitied it should be Sarah.

She figures she should go back downstairs. She won't be able to sleep with him still there. Going down is harder than going up even though gravity is on her side. Her fingers slide on the banisters, still smooth as silk even though she hasn't revarnished them since they bought the house. The ring on her right hand clicks on the wood and the skin stretched around it throbs. She should have taken it off but by now she's as stuck with it as she is with the man outside. She should have thrown it off the end of the pier. But he would have probably found it and returned it.

She moves to the kitchen window and scans the glass for a good projectile. Settles on a dried water streak that looks like a sludge of paint above him. He's still wet. She hasn't seen him dry for many months.

He's standing on the pavement but has turned his attention to slowly wringing out his sleeves, the bottoms of his trousers and his tie in one tight twist. He doesn't have shoes on. Otherwise he'd probably be pouring the water out of them like in a cartoon.

The sun is beginning to set and casts him in a yellow light. He coughs suddenly and a spurt of water flies out of his mouth. He wipes across his face ineffectually with one wet sleeve.

The light makes his skin look bluer and paler at the same time. She thinks she can see watery veins stand out like little rivers. His eyes are the same wan grey though they are lined with red. If he didn't look so sad she might not feel for him so much.

"I'm sorry," she says, suddenly.

"Me too," he says, water burbling out from between his algaed teeth. He walks backwards towards the pool. His jacket appears to have vanished from the water. The sun is almost down now and she holds her breath as he smiles at her, sadly, that killer smile, and jumps backwards, arms and legs straight as a penguin, into the swimming pool.

The skies are dark blue now and she cannot make out his shape underwater. Her eyes are watering. She walks over to turn the light on in the kitchen and when she returns to the window the pool is empty again. He'll probably be back tomorrow.

If only he had been wearing a different suit when he dove off the pier to try to rescue the struggling child. Maybe one she had picked out for him. Or if he hadn't left his shoes there, on the warped wood by the candyfloss stand. So that they were the only dry thing she had left to carry home.

She should get rid of the pool. But she probably won't. It's summer after all. There's still time to decide to go for a swim.

And the baby might enjoy the pool. It could meet him there, wave its chubby legs and arms in greeting and he might never have to get out of the water again. Because she's not sure the fabric of that suit should be repeatedly dampened and then dried. Better to stay luscious and dark like a black seal than fade under the summer sun.

Aaron Hubbard

Aaron Hubbard is from Kentish Town in London. As a child he wanted to be either a writer or a sumo wrestler, but his lightning-fast metabolism precluded him from pursuing the latter career. He studied first at Goldsmiths, then at the London College of Communication where he received his Masters degree in Scriptwriting. Aaron spent several years working as a development executive in the UK film industry, and is now focusing on his own script and prose projects. He lives in London with his wife and zero children.

Young Fairbrook

Young Fairbrook snared idle grouse on Sundays after church. So help her god. Squished and snapped the necks, under heel, blood stained and tattered her Sunday best. Easy pickin so they said, easy pickin. Nothing doing on Sundays. The other girls would play tag in the forest. Cut potatoes. Feed stock. Menfolk would mast pyres and spread gasoline, what with god coming to town. Ain't no telling Fairbrook 'bout god. She whispered the bad stuff. Some said she fell from her Mama and cracked her head, all gooey and soft. Didn't feel pain. Ain't no man talk heavy or share eyeline with her, not never.

Grouse tasted bad, brittle and dusty. Infected. She ate it under the pale moon. Next to the lumberyard. Scooped at the entrails, hawk-like squatting on her up-turned toes. Blood from her thighs, washed away and skinny dipped in the water. Floating like a bruised peach. Mama said there ain't no washing her. No bayou, lagoon or lake. That's what Mama said.

It was mean and fast. Humping in the back of the Model T. Junk didn't run. Gasoline weren't the problem neither. Mama said the plumbing was bust. Parked deep in the winter, frozen to the copse. Men hollered all but Sundays. Out they'd come, coal-trodden and mucked. Swinging pickaxes and slapping jokes. They'd lunch and linger. Form a queue. Four, five. Never more than six. Passul kept count. He was the watch-clock.

Sometimes they wouldn't muck her, but those days were hardly ever.

Didn't feel pain, they said. Passul. Mama. The men. Fell out her Mama and cracked her head. She whispered the bad stuff, but that was more than expecting. Lob-head, the girls hollered, from behind the church, keen and hidden to their knees. Day of rest, the Pastor told her as he smiled to church. She'd walk idle in the creek. Talked to god, whoever was listening. Inside they'd kneel and pray, sing holy and clasp. Then they'd dissipate and eat while Fairbrook snared her grouse.

Mama had taken a man. Gruff and brittle, panting in chase of jissum. No manners. Mama cooked slop weekly in a large pot. Served up with meat. Sometimes meat was out, which case he'd be eager for dishing a beating. Mama didn't mind much. Least she had a man. They'd go walking in their best, seen to be seen. All she ever wanted. Fairbrook didn't do no walking or talking with Mama or her man. Sometimes she'd scoop a handful of slop, careful not to burn herself. Under the stairs, hidden with her slop, licking her hands clean. One time Mama caught her, upsided her with a cold iron.

Every fortnight Passul would help the Pastor with the collections. Call round with a wooden bowl and god in their heart. When it rained Fairbrook kept busy with an umbrella, careful not to get the Pastor wet. Money went to the Pastor for his godly work, but Passul got his fill for helping too. And in the rain at least Fairbrook didn't have to sit sprawled in the Model T. Though she sometimes sat closed door in the church for Passul and the Pastor. Godly work.

Mama didn't go putting money in the Pastor's bowl. Didn't like Fairbrook wasting her talents. She couldn't be cleaned. No bayou, lagoon or lake. Nor no god. Mama always said she was a broken child, falling sudden and hollow like a vessel. Ain't no point in sustenance for a vessel. Instead Mama would drink her god money on wine and fall naked into bed. Easy pickin for her man. Those nights Fairbrook would sleep out back in the wet soil. Drift off and dream of the creek.

Passul was taken ill. Sat upright and green. They tried but he was too lost. The Pastor was called for last rites and soon after he was buried. They called on Mama 'cause she was only one save Passul who talked sense with Fairbrook. Ain't no one wanted a free-for-all. Voted for a new clock-watch. And she obliged. First lady allowed near the Model T, rapping knuckles in chase of jissum. Harsher than Passul. Regimented. Seven, eight, nine men a day. Didn't feel pain, she said.

Afterwards Fairbrook would bathe in the creek, notwithstanding the biting current. Cross-legged and private, this was a moment to herself. Passul hadn't cared, but Mama felt duty to watch. Called Fairbrook a lob-head and cautioned her against slipping and drowning, else Mama'd be out of pocket. Now Passul was buried Mama was accustomed to getting a bigger share. No right in not keeping fit your prize turkey, she'd say.

Pastor didn't like it. Started proselytising. Where in sense was the right that Mama took more while Passul's widow sat bone-dry? Mama didn't like slack-jawed talk, specially 'bout her business affairs. Only right in keeping balance, she said nasty things 'bout what the Pastor and Passul had been doing. Sure enough there was truth to it, Fairbrook knew too rightly. But no one went asking her.

Town called a meeting. Women stayed at home, excepting Mama who was there to fight her corner, and Fairbrook, out of orders from Mama. The Pastor hazed any ideas of homosexuality in the church, forcing the truth out of Fairbrook 'bout their times in the vestry. Talked proud 'bout Passul's widow. Charity. How Mama never tipped his collections. That Mama had a man anyway, wasn't needing an income. Crowd showed mighty agreement with the Pastor. He had god on his side. But Mama had Fairbrook. Mama said if she wanted her fair share she'd take her fair share, else she'd keep Fairbrook home. After she said her piece the men swaggered and joked, told the Pastor ain't no point in fixing something that ain't broke.

Mama and her man drank in cheer. Chased jissum in their cot. Spoke of Fairbrook while she slept in the wet soil. No pain, they said, she don't feel no pain. Somewhere that night they found the idea to make 'em rich. Simple maths. They spread word. Tidied her room up, real nice. Didn't take long for house guests to make noise. Even drew in some of the retired folk. On Saturdays they'd get outsiders too. Men from the next town. Ain't no one was turned away.

Sunday morning Fairbrook walked her Sunday best to the creek, got cross-legged and skinny. Thought she were alone, but Mama weren't nowhere near the church. She stood by the creek and hollered Fairbrook. Snapped her order to get dry. Some men had travelled from down the mountain. Fairbrook pretended not to hear so well. Her mind was settled on bathing and hunting. Nothing doing on Sundays. But Mama weren't so agreeable on this. Took a reed and whipped Fairbrook into shape.

First man went eager. Full of vigour and hootch. Said he ain't ever laid with someone so pretty. Second man was older. Gauche and unromantic. Forced sodom on her. She hailed a protest but Mama and her man were best counting their money to care. Afterwards it struck Mama that she could have gone charged extra, seeing as the men weren't local and didn't know better.

Fairbrook was given some slop and half a root beer, then was flanneled clean and shown to two more men. Travelers. Dirty. Ungodly men, lessing they'd attended midnight service. This time Mama charged extra. In eagerness to save money the two men shared Fairbrook at either end.

Fairbrook ain't never asked god for nothing, but that night she clasped tight and talked slack-jaw bout her Mama. Asked god to help her forgive her Mama. Next morning the fire was still in her belly. Seeing as god hadn't done diddly, Fairbrook thought it were only christian to help herself.

Mama served up slop and meat for her man, only there weren't no meat to be serving. She swore the meat'd gone missing, but that didn't stop her man beating on her. Next day she was the colour of barberry gin, and her head felt just as dizzy. Granted, Mama weren't the smartest of god's creatures, but it didn't take her long to piece the pieces.

Mama gripped her iron, but Fairbrook weren't sleeping in her cot. Nor outside neither. Little bitch went bathing on the creek, said Mama's man. Sure enough, Fairbrook was found, cross-legged and private, supping from her palmed hands. Mama hollered a whole bunch of swears. Kicked her boots and waded in. Tried taking a piece out of Fairbrook with the iron. But Mama weren't countin' on Fairbrook fighting back. What with her practice hunting grouse, didn't take Fairbrook long to drown Mama in the lake.

Ain't no one seeing Fairbrook after that. Some said her body was lost in the current. Others whispered she'd been torn apart by wolves. Ain't no one thought on putting out a search party. Finally one of the younger girls suggested it. Menfolk laughed at this girl telling them what to do. Then the rumours started. The girl was soft in the head. Didn't feel no pain, they said. Didn't feel no pain.

Jack Hughes

Jack Hughes was born in Romford in 1976 and has lived in Hampshire since 1990. Writing since childhood, he began writing novels in 1998. He has a BA in History, and an MA with Merit in Creative Writing from the University of Portsmouth.

Aside from writing, he has also trained as an RNLI lifeboatman, a TA soldier, and has written articles on maritime history for the BBC. In April 2013 he staged his first writing event, Pompey Writers, celebrating the rich literary culture and heritage of Portsmouth from Dickens to the present day.

The Montclair Redoubt

The mist came down, a gentle shroud covering the marionettes on the wire. Henry grew tired of watching them. The day before the stringless puppets in the middle distance were the men of the Dorsetshires, all filled with excitement at the prospect of cheap drink and friendly girls in the village. They went out as ordered; walking slowly with bayonets fixed, gas masks on. No one faltered. Their hopes would've lifted when they reached the wire unchallenged, thinking this was going to be the breakthrough. This time they'd get through, Henry could hear them telling themselves, they'd all be home by Christmas. That was how it always began. He knew the fishermen were waiting patiently with guns trained on their great steel keepnet. The order went up, they closed their eyes. And Hiram Maxim's ingenuity did the rest. At daybreak the Dorsetshires were there beyond the redoubt; ragged scarecrows Henry saw hanging from metal thorns.

The dug-out lacked everything; food, water, and hope. Inside sat a deaf lance-corporal and a half-frozen private; two living remnants in a company already dead with two full magazines for one broken rifle, a Maxim without bullets, and a broken-bladed bayonet. They were no longer holding the Montclair Redoubt, just biding time in its shelter, hoping the relief column would get to them first. In the twilight he'd seen them. The enemy. They weren't bothering to hide anymore; bold enough to smoke in his view, singing songs in foreign tongues, eager for dawn and their coming victory. Soon they would be coming for them, marching over Dorsetshires' bodies and past the shell-hole crypts to the sandbags. "We really should've gotten something in, if we'd known they were coming," Henry joked. The private, shivering beneath his freezing blanket of mud, didn't laugh or speak. Not that Henry would have heard. To the left of the redoubt he could see the outline of dead trees on the shell-chewed hill Lieutenant Morris waxed lyrical about the night before. Almost in sight of Agincourt, he'd said but nobody had listened. Cheap booze and friendly girls was all they wanted to hear about. The lieutenant taught history before the war, had married his childhood sweetheart on the day war was declared, had a younger brother in the Navy and a well-read copy of War of the Worlds that never left his side. He made it as far as the wire.

On his way back to the sandbags around the Maxim, Henry winced as something dug into his hand. Silhouetted figures began to move beyond the wire, steam-driven engines breathing thin wisps of cloud, advancing unhurried past the scarecrows. The mist closed in, and they vanished. Another joke at the ready, Henry smiled. The private wasn't shivering anymore. He just sat motionless as Henry lay back against the sandbags, spent, defeated. Shapes came out of the mist, and his last thoughts turned to prayer. Then to surprise when he saw what was digging into his hand.

Captain Walpole-Duggan sighed. His diary lay before him, pencil at the ready as it had been for nearly an hour. Recording the lives of soldiers was his business; the letter of condolence, and the daily report as familiar to him as the seasons to the oak that grew in his Wickham garden. So why was this any different? He'd heard such things around the Officers' Mess and dismissed them without a thought, but what was he going to tell them about the Dorsetshires and the Montclair Redoubt? Should he tell them about the enemy who lay slain but woundless around its sandbags? Or about the lance corporal who lay before them with only a broken rifle. And a five-hundred-year-old arrowhead.

Alison Love

Alison Love's short stories have appeared in several magazines including *The New Writer*, as well as in two anthologies published by Serpent's Tail. Her first novel, *Mallingford*, published by Black Swan, was described in *The Times* as 'the sort of book that reminds one why people still like reading novels', while her second, *Serafina*, set in 13th century Amalfi, was published through an Arts Council scheme. She has Literature degrees from the University of York and King's College London, and she has worked in the theatre, television and public relations.

Sophie Stops the Clock

It was cold in Vienna; too cold to snow, the servants said, huddled in their steaming jackets around the black kitchen stove. In the gardens of the Rofrano palace the late roses were leathery with frost. They had drained the fountains to stop the pipes from cracking.

In her bedroom the Countess Rofrano lay nestled in a heap of goose down pillows. 'Is it snowing yet?' she asked, as the chambermaid brought in her cup of chocolate.

Angelika shook her head. 'No, madam, not yet. The sky is bright blue. But it will snow, Gustav says, before the day is out. There's an icy wind blowing straight from Russia. You can hear the howl of wolves in it.'

Sophie smiled. 'Don't be silly, Angelika. You have no idea what Russia's like. It's a very civilised country. At least, the parts of it that the Count and I saw were very civilised. Everyone spoke French.' She took a foamy mouthful of chocolate. 'Is the Count still at home?'

'No, madam. He has gone to the Marschallin von Werdenberg's.'

Over the rim of her cup Sophie watched the maid fold back the shutters to let in the brittle winter sunlight. Oktavian, Sophie's husband, went to the Marschallin's every day, mooching about the draughty Werdenberg palace like a discarded lover. Marie-Thérèse – the Marschallin – was dying. Everyone in Vienna knew that. She greeted her visitors from her *chaise longue*, her face stiff and white with make-up.

'Angelika,' said the Countess, 'fetch my lotion, will you? Then you can bring my yellow dress.'

The tall windows rattled in the wind. Sophie poured the lotion into her cupped palm. The skin was rucking – a little, not much – on the back of her hands, and she wanted to nip that slackness in the bud. Fifteen years ago, when they were first married, Oktavian had laughed at her. Why are you women so obsessed by your looks? he asked, sprawling on the counterpane as she sat so gravely before her mirror. My cousin Marie-Thérèse is the same. Sometimes she stops the clock at night, to make the hours stand still.

Sophie smelt the rose-scented lotion. That's different, she had said. Of course Marie-Thérèse wants to stop the clock. She's getting old.

Angelika brought out the yellow dress.

'Nice and tight now, Angelika,' said Sophie. If it snows, she thought, while Angelika was straining at her laces, if it snows I shall wrap myself in honey-coloured furs and drive into the countryside. My sleigh bells will jingle like coins in a pocket, and the villagers will point at me, and say, there goes the beautiful Countess Rofrano. Perhaps Oktavian will come with me. He always used to come with me, when we were first married. He used to hold my hand under the rugs, and beneath the leather of his glove and the kidskin of mine I would feel his fingers tight and strong, and I would believe that we could go on driving for ever.

The memory made Sophie's throat ache. She turned to see the coiffeur arrive, with a wig on a wooden block, rolled and curled for powdering. Behind him Gustav, her major-domo, loomed in his scarlet coat.

'Baron von Arnim has called. He asks if you will see him.'

The Countess pictured Rudolf standing in the morning room, the corners of his elegant mouth turned down. For the last ten years she had had a string of cavaliers, well-born young men who claimed to be in love with her. Their ardour filled Sophie with a mild, rather frivolous intoxication, like the feeling she got after drinking a glass or two of champagne. There was no impropriety, no physical grossness of any kind; she simply found it entertaining to have the company of these idolatrous boys. Oktavian was away so much, so often. At first he told her that he was with his regiment, then that he was hunting with his wolfhounds. After a while, though – two years, maybe three – he stopped pretending that he was anywhere but the Werdenberg place, stopped pretending that he was with anyone but the Marschallin.

'Tell the Baron I will see him in forty-five minutes,' said Sophie, and she sneezed gracefully as the coiffeur opened his perfumed box of powder.

The morning room was at the front of the Rofrano palace. When Sophie came here as a bride she had been enchanted by the view across Vienna, the tumult of carriages, the officers on their high-stepping horses, swords glinting in the sunlight. Hers had been a fairytale marriage. You could not imagine a more dazzling bridegroom than Oktavian, with his fine blond hair and his slim thighs. The very buttons on his tunic shone with the promise of glamour and rescue. And they were in love, nobody could deny that. Oktavian had snatched her from the fortune-hunting baron whom her father had chosen, the man she had so nearly married. Sophie ran her fingertips along her tight-laced velvet waist. Not all women were so fortunate. As a girl Marie-Thérèse had been given to a thick-necked Field Marshal with bulging lascivious eyes. Even the Emperor's sister, delicious Antoinette, had been packed off to Paris as bride of the next king of France, whom everyone said was a dolt and a boor. The voice of Sophie's nasty old suitor came back to her, mellifluous, dissolute, singing under his breath.

Without me, without me, the nights are cold.

Sophie shivered. You never can tell what the future will hold. A week ago Oktavian had had another of his dreams. They woke him at dawn, flailing like a netted bird in the damp sheets. At first he had called for the servants to fetch Sophie, to sit with him and hold his hands, but now he did not trouble to disturb her. They were peculiar dreams. Sometimes he was rattling over cobbled streets in a cart, and in the distance, just out of sight, there was a whirring and a crashing, and at every crash the crowd roared, as his pack of hounds roared when they scented blood. Sometimes he was scrambling across a treacle-dark field, his boots weighed by mud, with the rat-tat-tat of muskets and yellow clouds drifting in the wind. The last dream was the strangest. In that dream queues of thin-faced people snaked towards a hut, while spiky figures stood watching. Oktavian said that was the worst dream, although he could not explain why. He could not explain it at all.

Rudolf was standing by the fireplace, just as she had imagined him, his face sharp with anxiety. He was the most ardent of all her cavaliers. She had thought that this time perhaps Oktavian would be jealous, but it seemed that Oktavian was never jealous. Rudolf swept across the room and kissed her hands.

'I thought you might not see me. I thought you might have shut up the house, on account of the Marschallin.'

'Not yet,' said Sophie. Her spirits rose to see his handsome haggard face. On the mantelpiece the Dresden clock chimed the half hour.

'They say she is dying,' said Rudolf, letting fall her hands. He spoke with the reverence so many voices acquired when they named Marie-Thérèse. Nobody ever said anything spiteful about the Marschallin. They never whispered that she drank too much wine at dinner, or that her breath smelt when you got close to her. Whenever she and Sophie met, at banquets or the gilded opera house, both in their puffballs of damask and satin, they would clutch one another and kiss the air extravagantly, and the Marschallin would say, dear Sophie, you make him so happy, and Sophie would want to say, but would not say, not as happy as you, dear Marie-Thérèse. You have his soul shut tight in your hand.

'It is impossible to think of Vienna without the Marschallin,' Rudolf said. 'I do not recall a time when she was not making my mother laugh with her stories, when she was not dancing at our New Year's ball.'

Sophie glanced out of the window. The old memory was returning, she could not stop it: fifteen years ago, as Oktavian stood frozen between the Marschallin and herself. It lasted an eternity, that moment, their three lives in the balance. And it was Marie-Thérèse who broke the spell. She pushed Oktavian gently – oh, so gently – in Sophie's direction. Such generosity, thought Sophie, such grandeur of spirit. How could I ever forgive it?

'She danced sublimely,' Rudolf was saying. 'Nobody danced like the Marschallin. Do you remember?'

The sky above the city was blue and immaculate. Perhaps at this moment, in the Werdenberg palace, Death was turning a solemn pirouette on the marble floor, offering his arm to the Marschallin. Stop the clock now, Marie-Thérèse, thought Sophie, stop the clock if you can.

'Rudolf – ' she said.

'Yes?'

'If it snows – when it snows – will you come driving with me in my sleigh?'

Rudolf frowned, tapping the ornamental sword at his thigh. 'By the time it snows the Marschallin will be dead. There will be no question of sleigh rides. You will be in mourning. I shall not see you for weeks. You will be shut up here with the Count.' He paused and said, in a quite different voice: 'His grief will be terrible.'

'Yes,' said Sophie calmly, 'it will be terrible.' She looked across at Rudolf. What if I threw myself upon him? she thought. What if I put his palm upon my breast, my tongue into his mouth? What if I lifted up my skirt and dared him to prove his passion, here, now? He would blench like a schoolboy. He would crumple.

Rudolf was gazing at her. There was a baffled expression on his face. Sophie smiled, and put out her small imperious rose-scented hand for him to kiss.

'And now, my dear,' she said, 'you had better go. My husband will be returning soon, and who knows what news he will bring?'

After Rudolf had left Sophie crossed to the fireplace, stretching her fingers to the blaze. With the Marschallin gone, she thought, perhaps we can start again. He will be bereft, I can comfort him, I am sure I can comfort him. She stared into the intricate red heart of the fire. It is not too late, we are both young, both handsome. He will come back into my bed, we might even have children. There is no reason in the world why we should not have children.

She sank into the little embroidered chair beside the fireplace. Outside the perfect sky was clouding over. Dense grey billows obscured the sun; the colours of the city blurred and faded. On the mantelpiece the Dresden clock was ticking. The room grew dark. Slowly, slowly, the first flakes of snow began to fall. They danced as they floated thickly downwards, blanketing the cobbles of the street, shrouding the stone Triton in the palace courtyard.

What roused Sophie was the clatter of a carriage beneath the window. Three doors slammed, one after another, and a man burst in, a plump red-faced man with a double chin. His nose was as raw as a radish. Sophie stared. The heat of the fire must have dazed her. Then she recognised the buttons on his tunic, bright gilt buttons which strained across his stomach.

'Sophie,' said Oktavian, 'it's Marie-Thérèse. The Marschallin – '

Sophie leaped from her chair. 'No,' she cried, 'don't tell me,' and reaching out she stopped the hands of the clock.

Erinna Mettler

Erinna Mettler's first book *Starlings*, an episodic novel set in Brighton, was published by Revenge Ink in 2011 and was longlisted for the Edge Hill Prize. She is a founding member of the spoken word co-operative Rattle Tales. Her stories have appeared in many journals and been performed at events such as Grit Lit, Ace Stories, Liar's League, and Word Theatre.

www.erinnamettler.com

What Me and Pa Saw
in the Meadow

'What is it?' I whisper.

Me and Pa spent the morning fishing in the Diamond Bank river and we are on our way home. We jus' walked through the Primavera forest, which is how come we didn't see it sooner. As we turn into the blue meadow there it is standing on the path a little way up hill. It stops us dead in our tracks and we stand on the edge of the grass staring at the thing blocking the route home. At almost quarter-day, with the sun nearing its most ultra-violet, I think I must be hallucinatin', but Pa holds up his hand, fingers splayed, in a silent hush.

From its vantage point on the path, the thing lifts its head and looks at us with big black eyes as deep as space. Its jaw, which is grindin' from side to side, stops and falls open, showin' tombstone teeth and crushed blue grass. Aqua saliva and pieces of grass dribble to the ground. My mouth is dry with fear. My heart beatin' so fast I can hear it outside my body. Those teeth look like somethin' from the horrors. I imagine those chompers bitin' into me, crushin' my cells and veins, and me dyin' right here from blood loss and infection – that's if it doesn't just gobble me and Pa up right now, bones 'n all. I silently cuss Pa for makin' me come all the way out here, so far from civilisation, with only Dawkin's Neons skittering the skies for company.

Pa likes to go fishin' at end week. We live right on sprawl edge, it's the only place we can afford, but it means we can be outsprawl quicker than most folks. We go fishin' early day, before sunrise and the cloudless sets in, and then come back in time for lunch so as not to be out in the tip heat, but today we stayed longer at the river because Pa was sure he'd get a bite.

Course, we never actually catch any fish. Fish aren't made to be caught. Fishin's suppose' to be jus' for fun, but Pa always says,' ya never know.' And there was this one guy down New Miami way, who landed a quawn fish as long as his arm. It was all over the news stream for days. He was real famous, Baxter Dartmouth III was his name. You couldn't close your eyes without seeing his smilin' face as he hugged that big ugly fish. Some said it was a throwback fish and that's how he caught it but they did tests on it and it was legit an all. They let him keep it too, on account of him being the first human to catch a fish in over 60 years. Now they use that photo to advertise fishing lines. Dartmouth's they're called, not that we can afford one, we jus' got TaiHam wire and a 3-D rod. Mind, they have nothin' but water down in New Miami so it must've bin easier for Baxter Dartmouth III to catch that fish than it would be for us to get one, but Pa says,' if he can do it we can, we just gotta keep tryin'.' An' it is true that if we did happen to catch one (hopefully an even bigger one) we wouldn't have to worry about credit no more (and Ma does worry about credit.) We'd be famous. We could move insprawl. It would have to be a pretty impressive fish though, now that Baxter Dartmouth III has set a precedent, and that's why Pa says we should try an' catch somethin' really rare, somethin' no-one's laid eyes on for a very long time.

The best fishin' grounds round about, the ones with the really rare fish, those ones are way outsprawl. That's how come me and Pa are out here in the blue meadows on a rest day, as far from the sprawl and the security pods as you can be without a vehicle. There's no stream cameras out here. Pa says walkin' is good for you, says, in the old days when he was a kid everybody walked everywhere. Says it's better for your cells than the hover plates. An' I do like to walk out here with Pa, away from the sprawl, even though it is usually almost too hot to think. But Ma frets. 'Be careful,' she says, 'anythin' could happen.' And today she's right.

The thing snorts and stamps its foot and I nearly jump from my skin. Its feet have two pointy dust-covered toes that look as hard as titanium. Its legs seem too thin to hold up its wide barrel body. It looks like it could crush us with that body, just land on us and roll the life right out of us. Maybe it's a robot? They have things like that on the funny streams; robots from outer space! Or maybe it's somethin' to do with the military? I edge behind Pa and cling to his arm, peerin' round his body. I'm sure that at any minute the thing will attack us and I wonder what I should do if it does. If it knocks Pa flat should I run, or would that be worse? Would it come after me and charge me down? But it just sneezes, bends its head into the blue grass, rips up a hunk of it and sets about chewin' again.

'Well I'll be,' says Pa.

He motions for me to sit and I find a big ol' diamond rock next to the meadow but I don't take my eyes offa the thing, not for a second. Pa sits next to me and his face is all crinkled up and smiley like it is when the Perseids blaze. I still keep the thing in sight but Pa's expression is makin' me feel less shaky. If he ain't scared I shouldn't be either.

'What is it Pa?' I ask.

He scratches his head.

'I saw one years ago when I was just an infant, couldn't have been no more than five. It was on display in the town cube. Looked just like this one. I remember it clear as day, constantly chewin' at grass.' He looks at me and winks. 'The grass was green back then son, not blue like now.'

Pa has mentioned this green grass thing before but I don't know as I believe him. I know they had green grass in Germanica but I never seen any pictures of it here in the CUSA, and Pa's only a hundred so I don't see how he canna' seen it.

'It's called a K-OW.'

'A k-ow?'

Rhymes with POW, I think to myself. I can feel my eyes get real wild despite the sun.

'Is it dangerous?'

Pa laughs.

'No son, it's not dangerous. Well that is, the individual k-ow ain't dangerous. See years ago, before the Disaster, there was k-ows in every field. You couldn't go anywhere outside the sprawls without seeing a k-ow. Millions of 'em, Big black and white lumps in every meadow, all chewin' away at that green green grass.'

'What were they for Pa?'

'Farming, son. You could get meat and milk from 'em and somethin' like Theal for shoes and clothes; it was made from the skin.'

'How's that Pa - didn't they have the vats back then?'

I have just completed Food Techno Level 8 so I know all about the utero vats and manusustenance.

'No son, food wasn't cultured then, came straight from the animal. No cloning either. The milk came from that dangly bit underneath and it wasn't flavoured like now. To get the meat they had to terminate the k-ow and cut it up. We have one of Grandpa's history files about it in the archive - Cattle Farming and Butchery for Begin…'

He sees my face and stops talkin'. I feel well and truly nauseous - terminated and cut up! Milk from inside an animal! Pa takes an atomizer from his backpack and I squirt it twice onto my tongue.

'You look like your cell glucose is down,' he says, 'you should eat somethin'.' He takes one of Ma's shrink-wraps from the bag and hands it to me. 'What is it?'

'Meat 'n' algae bread.'

I bite into it and immediately feel like I'm back home in our kitchen surrounded by smells from our food creator, and the horror of cutting up the k-ow doesn't seem so bad. Ma creates the best meat 'n' algae bread I ever tasted. She knows just what compounds to add and when and the whole thing comes out jus' perfect. Whenever, and wherever, I eat Ma's meat n algae bread I always feel like I jus' got a kiss on the forehead from her.

I swallow and take another bite, feeling calmer by the milli-flic.

'So what happened to the k-ows?' I ask with my mouth half full.

'Well they say the meat was delicious. The most unbelievable taste. Grandpa was always talkin' about how good it was, how juicy and soft. Melted in your mouth, he said, like the best meat times a graham. He said when it was cooking you could smell it for miles around and the dogs used to whine with anticipation it smelled so fine. He made it sound so good I always wished I coulda tasted it - just once. But this was before fat gobblers and targeted exercise pills and it was really bad for you. Clogged up your heart; made it so it couldn't beat proper. People only lived to around 80 years old then. Imagine that! Just 80 years old. But that wasn't all. K-ows ate fields full of grass every day and well, that much veggimat causes gas - y'know, in the belly.'

He makes an ass-fart sound with his lips and I can't help but laugh. Pa laughs too; there is just somethin' so funny about ass-farts. Probably because we're nervous about the k-ow, we laugh until our sides ache and I need another spray from the atomizer. Pa wipes his eyes and carries on. He likes talkin' bout the past, sometimes he sounds like our Urban Mythology facilitator Partner Price, but she says we shouldn't believe everythin' we hear from our families, that folks like to make things up, especially about the times before The Disaster. But when Pa talks he's just so convincin' I don't know what to think.

'They didn't have pills for breakin' up veggimat then and that many k-ows all ass-fartin' at once made the world smell and the ozone thinner. Some said the k-ows was responsible for the Disaster and they made it illegal to keep one unless it was in a laboratory with a license. We were lucky they stopped it when they did; otherwise we wouldn't have the pink sky and clean air we have now.'

I look at the beast chewin' the blue grass in front of us and feel kinda sorry for it.

'Where'd it come from?'

Pa shrugs.

'I streamed they have to keep one or two full clones in the factories for source cells. It must be one of those. There's that Meat Link bio-dome close to us, it musta' escaped from there. Higgs Boson knows how!'

Just then the k-ow stops chewin', looks directly at us and makes a loud and low noise the like of which I haven't even heard on the streams.

MEEEUUUNGGHH!

Then it falls down with a thud, frightnin' a cloud of Neons from the trees so they all scream for help as they fly away.

Me and Pa look at each other and then he goes over to where it lies. He takes his scanner from his pocket and holds it above the k-ow. After a minute it beeps the safe message. Pa crouches and puts his hand on the k-ow's body then looks back at me and shakes his head.

'It's alright,' he says, 'it's terminated. Probably the heat. There's no contamination. I think they need as much water as grass and there's no water out here, musta dehydrated. Come see.'

I'm scared, but I don't want Pa to know I am, so I walk over to it. The sun is as high as can be and the grass is still. I look down at the k-ow, black and white like solstice clouds, and stretch my fingers out to touch it. It's still warm, and as soft as Nap, but it's not breathin' and its eyes are shut. It looks so sad lyin' there - terminated. I ain't never seen anythin' terminated before.

'What should we do,' I ask. 'Should we get help?'

Pa takes his hat off and wipes the back of his neck with it.

'I don't think so son. Security might not believe we just found it. Traffickin' full clones is a serious offence, a hundred years or more in correction. With no security stream out here to prove we didn't take it, I don't think we should risk reportin' it.'

He's right, without stream proof they'd think the worst. You hear about it all the time, the authorities never take the word of ordinary folk. There's always people on the streams getting charged with citizenship violations. Sent away to the Correction State for years at a time. Most of 'em don't look like criminals but I guess they mus' be if they's on the streams but it's certainly not the sort of fame Baxter Dartmouth III got when he caught his fish an' it's not the sort of fame we was after when we set off this pre dawn either. Even if the guards didn't charge us for stealing a clone, there'd be months of surveillance and when you're under surveillance everybody watches you, the guards, family, neighbours even people you don't know! And besides, Ma would hate it; she likes to keep our business ours.

'Are we just going to leave it then?' I ask. 'Pretend we didn't see it?'

'Well now that seems a bit disrespectful, dontcha' think? Such a wonder deserves better than just being left to decay.'

I'm confused. We're not gonna report it and we're not gonna leave it.

'What are we gonna do with it then Pa?'

He grins and stands up.

'Cattle Farming and Butchery for Beginners,' he says. 'First, we go get the solar jeep.'

Amanda Oosthuizen

Amanda Oosthuizen is a writer, musician and teacher from Hampshire, UK. She has won prizes and been shortlisted in various contests, most recently the *Litro* Poland/Bruno Schulz Competition where, freakily, her story, *Gloves of Gdańsk*, was displayed at King's Cross Station. Her novel extract, *The Glorious Dolores*, was performed with aplomb in March 2013 by Liars' League in London and her novel, *Cherry Wood Box*, was highly commended in the 2012 Yeovil Prize. Stories-in-print include *Litro* via the superb *Polish Cultural Institute*, *The Lampeter Review* and *Scraps*, the National Flash Fiction Day 2013 Anthology. Links to a plethora of online work at www.amandaoosthuizen.com.

Poison Hands

Daisy is on the cliff edge, barefoot again. At 82, she's a frail, white fragment, teetering against the ice blue sky. I see her shoulders rock in the Atlantic wind, silvery hair flying in a wispy cloud. She stares at the waves. I should lock the door.

At sea, my fingers swelled from the sisal and fish gutting. Poison hands, we called it. The first time Daisy saw them, my wedding ring had sunk beneath the skin.

"Your finger will drop off, Lion." She sounded awestruck.

"It's fine." It hurt like hell. I leaned back on the sofa.

She fetched her bread knife. I kissed her neck and curled my arm round her waist.

"I'll have more than your finger." She sawed at the ring.

"We caught the biggest halibut you ever saw. Ten, twelve stone." I blinked at the pain.

She shook her head.

"True. I swear."

"Liar." She looked up through her lashes.

"And Brigsy nearly had his eye out on a cable."

"Sounds like him." Daisy had grown up on the same street as Brigsy and me but Daisy and I shared secrets.

When she'd cut through the gold, she parted the ring with her teeth and as she pulled it off, the skin pinched and I wanted to howl.

Three days later, she packed my clothes. I kissed her goodbye in her Mum's front room, threw the kit bags over my shoulder and marched down the dock without looking back.

Her toes hook over the edge of a slab of stone like a sea eagle's talons. Fifty feet below, the sea crashes onto rocks.

"You should put on your boots before you come out here."

As a gust sweeps up the cliff face laden with spray, I grab her arm. But even the wind with its cold salt pins doesn't disrupt her focus on the horizon. Memories can haunt and perturb but they're more precious every moment that passes.

I slip my coat round her shoulders and coax her from the edge. Her eyes are pale blue and teary but Daisy never cries. It's a January wind with ice teeth. The fish come down from the polar cap and lay their eggs on the continental shelf. Good fishing in January. Lots of fat fish.

Brigsy and I were fifteen when our dads took us down the docks and said 'here's a couple of galley boys for you'. We spent two days in our bunks while the weather stormed, smelling the stench of oranges and tobacco, stale fish and wet socks. With the ship creaking, the men gutting fish in the middle of the night, the constant rattle of steering chains, I thought I was going to die. The only thing that kept me going was pride. I didn't want Brigsy to see how bad I was. I watched him retch and topple.

"Just be careful." That's what I told Brigsy.

"The sea doesn't scare me. She's like your Daisy; I can wrap her round my little finger."

You never joke about the sea. Never. On the third day, mountainous waves rose over the rail like grabbing monsters, sweeping us off our feet, filling our thigh boots, leaving us cold for the rest of the day. We travelled at full speed 1500 miles to Bear Island, into Arctic waters to the fishing grounds. The spray froze. A blizzard covered the ship in solid snow. The men worked twenty hour shifts in half daylight, sweeping the seabed, hauling nets and gutting fish. They told us how a jagged cable cut a man in half. When the skipper made us crack ice off the cables with hammers, I put up with the pain in my hands.

The fourth day, the ship was shrouded in fog as we crept amongst icebergs, the air thick with silence except for the murmur of the engine and the bergs squealing and popping and creaking. It became a different world. Heaven.

Sometimes we worked in the fish hold. The men chucked cod down the chute and we covered them in ice. Even though they'd been gutted, they twitched. Some spewed their guts. Brigsy made them jump on each other. We had a laugh. Brigsy turned harsh work into a good time.

By the time Daisy and I had been engaged for a year, Brigsy and I were closer than ever. But one day, in the bunks during a storm, he grabbed the photograph I kept in my oilskins. Daisy in the fairground on a summer's night. He stared at it.

"She's turned into a bit of all right. Have you done her?"

I smacked him in the face. He wiped the blood with his arm and laughed.

The sky is turning purple and pink, with a touch of green high up. The Northern Lights in Icelandic waters, beyond Dogger Bank, twirl and flirt like girls in long green dresses, dancing in the sky as if the night is full of madness.

"What are you doing, Daisy?" I keep talking to her, but she rarely finds words to talk back. It's the stagnant silences that I find unbearable. On a good day she'll mumble incoherently and pace the house, agitated, moving things from place to place as if she's searching for the pattern that will make everything fit together again. I think she's closest to what she's looking for on the cliff edge. That's why I decided to keep the door open but...

"Waiting."

"What for?" I take her palm. It's lined with tiny creases. Her body's all rattling bone and chicken skin, not plump and pink like it used to be. Her hands are silvery, almost transparent. I trace the letter D. She blinks.

"Lion." She shakes off my hand. "Lion will be back. He always comes back. Not all of them do." It's more words than she has spoken in weeks.

"I know." I hug her. She smiles, her face alight like she's young again and then she droops, her skin collapses, darkens and she's stricken and shivering.

"Lion always comes back," I say.

She raises her chin and presses her lips together. I kiss her cheek and she shudders. Three days home and three weeks at sea, we kept so much from each other. No. I don't want her to remember everything.

I lead her to the kitchen chair, towel her toes and clasp her feet, like two slim doves, between my hands. For a second she rests her cheek against my shoulder and I grin, stroke her head. She smiles. I slip her feet into woollen stockings and lace her boots tight, stiffening her ankles, so she won't fly off the cliff.

By the time we were married, I'd become bosun. I handed my money to Daisy, so we had our own place, unlike Brigsy who still lived with his Mum. Brigsy splurged his pay at Rayner's on booze and getting laid and often, he'd come round ours for dinner. While I was home, I'd treat Daisy like a princess. She'd hire a washing machine and while my kit was drying on the line, I'd take her into town and treat her at The Golden Dragon and buy her jewellery, anything she wanted.

We'd been three weeks at sea and were homeward, close to Flamborough Head when a following sea climbed onto the ship, and she listed. Brigsy and I were whiling the storm in the bunkroom playing cards. I froze, bracing myself for the lurch as she righted but another wave followed. We felt her turn and then we were flung against the bulkhead amongst kit and oranges, tins and boots.

"Bloody hell!" Brigsy crawled to the door.

Water was pouring in. Perhaps it was fear or maybe the tumble but I couldn't shift a muscle. Brigsy waded back and dragged me out before the deck door slammed for good. We battled downwards, emerging as the ship turtled. I didn't think of home or Daisy. I just followed Brigsy climbing the rail underneath the ship, in the murk, making my breath last. That morning we learned to swim. It's not so hard when you have to.

Eventually they dragged us up in the life raft. She took four hours to sink and we lost five men. It changed my life. Five decent men gone. The thing was, I didn't go home. I spent two days on the whisky and staggered straight onto the new ship.

The next time I saw Daisy, three weeks later, she'd changed.

"I thought they'd made a mistake when you didn't come home."

"What did you expect?" I was too pig-headed to apologise.

"Then Brigsy came over and said you were at the pub."

"Brigsy was with me."

"You passed out. He came to check I was all right." She turned away. "I'm not settling for this, Lion."

I imagined Brigsy comforting Daisy.

"Haven't you got anything to say?"

"What do you want me to say? I'm sorry? Men were drowned at sea."

"You want to know what I think." She pulled the ring from her finger and threw it at me.

I was mad with Brigsy, mad with her. "I'm going out," I said.

"If you go out, I'm coming with you."

She ran after me. I went into Rayners and left her outside. I drank while she leant against the wall, staring at the dock. And then Brigsy was leaning next to her smoking a cigarette. I watched her take one from his packet and Brigsy lighting it, leaning into her hair like he'd been there before and her eyelashes batting at him. I saw her let out a long sigh and Brigsy take her hand.

I stayed until closing time, wondering how often Brigsy had been round our house. I remembered glances, the way his hand rested on the table almost touching hers, how she laughed too long at his jokes. I dragged myself home and slept on the floor with my head on my kit bag and left early without even talking to her. I found her ring under the stove and kept it in my tobacco tin.

From then, I watched Brigsy. He was smaller than me with wide green eyes that showed nothing except his joking. One day, we found ourselves in a strong south east gale in the Long Forties, the worst I'd seen with climbing, mountainous waves streaked with foam, spume flying off the crests. One moment the bow was rearing up and the next, we were dropping, crashing into the trough with a sickening thud. I was on the bridge. Everyone else was below, sleeping off the storm. We'd hauled a piece of old aeroplane in the nets and I saw Brigsy clambering over the fuselage amongst slices of rusted metal, kicking off his sea boots for a better grip.

I saw the swell, knew we were going to list. All it took was a few seconds. He checked the lashings on the plane but he didn't see the wave. The sea rose like a moving mountain. I knew it was going to crash on him, suck him into the swell. I didn't shout. All I could think of was his head in Daisy's hair and all the times he'd been alone with her since. I remembered how he'd dragged me out of the bunk room and I didn't even throw a line. The bow dipped, solid water came over the rail, the ship rolled on the swell and he was down, slipping into the plane amongst the broken metal sharp as knives.

I jumped on deck, fought through waist-deep water and pulled him out, all of him except his toes.

Brigsy couldn't take rolling seas after that so they put him in the galley as ship's cook shovelling up battered cod and porridge. And one day, years later, after I'd made skipper, he folded up his apron, laid it on the deck and dived overboard.

I take Daisy to the car. A flock of gulls wheel and dive on the air currents.

I drive to St Andrew's docks, the old docks, and park on a patch of pitted concrete. The sun is almost gone. Plastic bags flap in the brambles like terns in the nets; beer cans glint in the gulley. We walk tiny steps through long, yellow grass. Water slaps against the rotting wood of the old lock gates.

I sit her on an iron bollard where we used to moor the ships while I climb down into the dock. It's filled with rubble. I pull out the old tobacco tin that's been jammed between two bricks for more than forty years.

"I have something for you," I say.

It takes her a moment to sort out the words and she looks me over before stretching out her hand.

I knock the tin on the concrete to loosen the rust and prise off the lid with my knife. She watches, her head so close I can feel her breath on my hand as I take out the rings and try to imagine what she might be seeing. She rubs her finger along the sharp edge of the split gold and walks away through the long grass.

Rachel Peters

Rachel Peters is currently residing in her hometown of Richmond, Virginia, where she has recently left a career in education to devote her time fully to her writing. She is a graduate of Rhodes College in Memphis, Tennessee, and she has an academic background in classical studies, English and psychology. *When You Check in to 3 West* is her first published work.

When You Check in to 3 West

I.

It will be late – after midnight – by the time they've given you a tetanus booster and found a nurse to escort you down impossibly long hallways. You will carry your belt, your socks and shoes, your wallet in a plastic bag, and you will talk about nothing so you don't have to hear your steps echoing down the linoleum.

When you enter the ward, you will meet Maria. She will be calming and friendly and will give you a pen and a notebook. You will be eternally grateful to her for that. She will ask you where you see yourself in ten years. You will fill out forms, and two more nurses will take your blood pressure. They will give you a number for an empty room, and you will be grateful for that, too.

It will take a few days before you get used to the doctor who takes blood pressures at five in the morning, before you stretch your arms out from under the quilt and keep dreaming. The first night you will sit up, say something you hope is polite. The doctor will say, in an accent that might be Pakistani, don't get up. The machine will say, beep beep. The deflating cuff will say, shhh. And that will have to do for a lullaby.

The quilt on the bed will be enough to keep you warm, but not enough for you to feel safe. In a few days you will find where they keep extras, and you will sneak three more into your room. It will take time to learn the rules, to find your confidence.

No joke, the tetanus shot will hurt.

They will call you for breakfast at eight, and since you will have no clothes or toothbrush you will walk right out, but everyone else will already be gathered around three tables still in their pajamas and hospital gowns. You will hesitate, cowering, peering out from behind a door, and then you will walk in and ask if you can take an empty chair.

The empty chair will be across from Victoria. You'll have to read her name off her bracelet. She will remind you of a mouse, the way she pushes the food around on her plate until Stella says, "You've got to eat, honey," and then Victoria will lean across the table. "They won't let you out if you don't eat."

II.

Angie will sit to the right of the doctor who leads Sunday group sessions. She will joke about how her upcoming ECT might cause enough brain damage for her to forget how depressed she is, and about washing Ryan's dirty socks until Emmaline interjects, "Angie was raped, y'all," and then Angie will smile, and then she will cry. And then Stella will stand up, set the tissues on her walker and bring them over to Angie. Angie will blow her nose loudly, wipe her smeared mascara with the dirty tissue, smile and say, "Hey doc, I think that's it for me today." The doctor will smile. "Thank you for sharing with us, Angie. And how are you today, Victoria?"

Mark will make you nervous at first. He can't sit still unless he's fallen asleep in group with his head thrown back and his mouth open, snoring. You will find out that he went off his meds and even before that, that he and his wife were having trouble. That he found himself lying on his living room floor, holding his gun and crying. He's in something not very memorable, and she teaches English in a maximum security juvenile detention facility. You will be able to tell by the way he talks about her, and how often, that he used to love her. Remembers loving her the way you all remember loving. From before you went numb.

Most of you are voluntary – whatever that means anymore, but Jun is on a seventy-two hour hold. All she will say, for seventy-two hours is, "I not kill self! If I kill self I not say kill self!" The therapist will not understand her through her limited English tinged with Japanese, but you will. Her words and what they mean.

Paula will check out the same day you check in, but you will remember how strangely efficient she seemed. She wears her hair short, has put on make-up, and she will talk about her addiction like it's just plain business. She's the only addict on the ward; at least the only drug addict. Because aren't you all addicted to something?

When it is your turn, you will say things – it doesn't matter what things – that are true, but when you say them, you know they aren't the truth. Eventually you will learn the difference.

You will not be allowed to go outside – insurance reasons – and so Emmaline will have to be your sunshine. Your eighty-year-old mother, grandmother and childhood best friend all rolled into one, exiting the room every five minutes with an "excuse me; I have to go empty my bladder." You will never find out what brought her to 3 West. All she says is, "I want to stay happy and not depressed, just the way that I am. I'm Miss America." And she is.

The first day you will cry. You will cry because you are tired, because your wrist hurts, because you miss your bed and you do not know what to expect here. You will cry because you are still here, because today is a day you did not plan on having and it does not feel like a gift. Because you let your husband down. And yourself. And you do not yet have the words that need saying.

There will be a lot of tears.

III.

You will be surprised to find out that the way they call you up for meds is not like in the movies. No organized lines with nurses who hand you one cup with pills and one with water and then check under your tongue to make sure you swallowed them. You will find out that the pills are completely voluntary, which is funny because the only thing anybody on 3 West wants is more meds. But you can't have Advil or caffeine or nicotine patches without a doctor's order. You will ask your husband to sneak chocolate covered espresso beans, but that won't be until the third day and by then the headache will have passed.

Your brother will be the first person to call you. He will ask, "why didn't you call me?" You will not say, "because you might have helped me." And then he will ask, "Was it because the Spiders played such a crappy game?" And you will think how nice it would be to have a reason.

You should make sure your husband doesn't bring you your favorite track sweatshirt. The string is not removable and they will make you cut it out if you want to keep the sweatshirt. It's your favorite, so you will send it home, but you're going to lose that job anyway when they find out about this.

You will eat so frequently that you will forget the feeling of an empty stomach. You will learn to jump up when you hear "Kitchen's open!" but you will make up for hunger in thirst. The air is dry and the pills soak all the moisture from your mouth and throat. The nurses will scold you for trying to get snacks for Emmaline and for Victoria. She will not understand how badly you need to find a purpose.

"I'm trying to be as helpful as I can, so they'll let me out," Ryan will whisper as he stands to answer the phone.

It will not occur to you that this might not work until the third person asks you if you've been here before. You tell one of the shrinks, "I don't want to be those people," and he corrects you, "You don't want to be where they are." But you meant what you said. You still mean it.

At six each evening, and at two on weekends, there are visiting hours. Ninety minutes you will all look forward to all day, but then you will watch the clock until you no longer have to face husbands, wives, mothers, fathers, siblings. You will not remember how to act, what to say. You will wish that you had shoes, a belt. You will feel so awkward without them.

Your father will arrive unannounced and uninvited. They will tell you, "A man who says he's your dad wants to come see you, but he doesn't have your room number. Should we let him in?" Your face will reveal your panic and disappointment. "Who told him?" you will ask your sister.

He will try to relate to you, will tell you about his depression. He will say, "Depression is pure pain. The ads on TV don't tell you that." And he will be right about that. He will tell you that the hardest part is how no one understands, and he will be right about that too. And then he will tell you about turning depression into academic study. About marking your mood on a musical scale and watching its ups and downs. About the power that comes from naming your enemy.

He will tell you that every action has an equal and opposite reaction. "You have to bounce." And you will see how hard he is trying, but still, when he leaves, no one will believe that he isn't your psychiatrist, even if you do look just like him.

Your mother will finally drop in on the third day, will not stay long and will not call you the day you are released. Months later she will point out how unfriendly you were to her when she visited. And although her priorities will not surprise you, be prepared because that will hurt.

Really hurt.

You will not have the energy to read in here, but you will appreciate – and later cherish – the copy of Jewish Activism your brother brought from his job at the Holocaust museum. Your sister-in-law will bring Chelsea Handler; she doesn't know you at all, but you will love her for the gesture. Without reading, you will have to take up pointillism. You will sketch a dozen trees, leaves red and orange and yellow. And a spider you saw in a dream. It will be a long time before you can look at words on a page.

IV.

Your doctor will come visit you after it has been made clear to you that he doesn't do hospital stays. There's a different doctor on your wristband, but you will get a new one later. A wrist band, not a doctor. You will be embarrassed that he is seeing you like this. You will pull your husband's sweatshirt down over your hands and tuck your shoeless feet underneath you. You are still wearing slipper socks.

He will tell you a story about cockroaches. How when he lived in an infested apartment, he used to catch them in a jar, as many as he could. Left it out when a date came over, though. "I have a sick sense of humor," he will say, and you will try to smile. "But that doesn't do anything for clinical depression," he will add.

He will say, "Cutting doesn't bother me. Neither does suicidality, but if you want my advice: don't."

He will say, "I can't keep you here until you get better, but I can keep you here for awhile. Do you feel safer here?"

You will tell him that your husband feels safer.

The nurse who pulls the bandage off for wound consult will look relieved. She will smile and say, "that should heal up fine," and she will move on to the next person. It will make you feel insignificant and ashamed.

You all will hate the chimes that play every time a baby is born downstairs in labor and delivery. You will be filled with envy, astounded that anything good can happen in this world, and appalled that anyone could bring a child into this mess and then play chimes to celebrate it.

Ryan will teach you that laughter is the way to cope in here, so you will joke about Emmaline running off with your husband, about Ryan having to give up his shotty, even though he tried to hang himself. "If I were gonna do it, I wouldn't use a gun." "Don't tell them that," you will say, "or they'll make you give up belts and shoelaces."

You will make crazy jokes. You will find power in the word "crazy" and in the taunts about not cooperating and being sent to 2 West – that's where the real crazies are, the people you really don't want to be.

V.

The third day. Ryan and Katie, both Marks, Carrie and William, Isabel and Alexis will check out. Victoria leaves AMA.

You will wonder how anyone could be better in five days. How can anything be better in two more days? You will start to think that you will never leave. You will panic, and then you will realize that it doesn't matter. You will become just like everyone else who says, "I might leave tomorrow." And tomorrow just doesn't come. You will say to no one in particular, or maybe to the therapy dog, "If I left today it would be the same old shit." The dog will wander on to comfort someone else.

With so many people gone, the ward will be quiet. The phones will seem so loud. And the TV and the beeping when Emmaline gets her blood pressure checked or Frank has his blood sugar tested. Eventually those sounds will quiet, and maybe that's when you're ready to get out. Or maybe it's just when insurance stops paying.

VI.

Karen will appear on the fourth day. You will notice first her Mickey Mouse sweatshirt. You will wonder why she would grab that on her way out the door; why she would choose that to die in. It will seem inappropriately youthful, hopeful. But don't you all have your security blankets in here? Ryan with his Soundgarden t-shirt, Janie carrying her unicorn Pillow Pet in spite of repeated scolding from the day nurses. You have your notebook.

Second, you will notice the bandage on her wrist. You sit next to her at medicine group. You will notice that, like you, she takes notes, and that, unlike you, she asks questions. You will be surprised at how invested she is in her recovery.

She will be so excited for exercise group, and you will feel so silly holding a ball over your head and writing the alphabet. You will watch the door intently; your psychiatrist cannot see this. But you will try to enjoy the experience, and you will pretend that it even resembles exercise. You will be annoyed when it makes you sweat, but it doesn't get your heart pumping.

There will be visiting hours again, and it will be clear how much distance there is between you and your husband, He will hold you too tight, and rub his finger back and forth on the same spot on your arm, and you will tell him he is giving you an arm burn. You will be lying about that. It doesn't hurt, not physically.

Someone else will come too. A sister, parent, brother. It doesn't matter who. You will wish you could spend time with them instead of comforting your husband like he's the one in here, and not you. But you owe him that, you will tell yourself. You will believe you owe him a lot, but at least he didn't have to hose blood out of the garage like Karen's husband.

There will be something on TV – a reunion for the cast of *The Color Purple*, unless maybe that's another day. It might be *NCIS*.

There will be another snack when they leave. There will always be another snack, and you will fill your giant plastic mug with ice water. You will miss that mug later. It was by your side for six days. It is so sturdy, and the lid fits so well, but it has the hospital name on it, and so you have to leave it behind. You will eat cereal with milk, or Fig Newtons, or ice cream and graham crackers. Sometimes animal crackers and peanut butter. But they are off-brand animals. They are all monkeys.

VII.

You will go to reflection group with Nurse Linda. You don't know her, but Angie will talk to her like an old friend. Linda will talk to you like you are a human being, and you will realize how much you have missed that. She will say things like, "You realize that doesn't make any sense, right?" or "If you don't like it, then stop doing it." She will hand out the poem she is supposed to be reading with you and then join you in complaining about the nurses on the morning shift.

Frank will not be at group, but he will approach Linda after, shouting because he is deaf and because he is an old bat.

"I am tired of being lied to and led around in this place!" he will shout, and you and Angie and Karen will pull chairs around the table to watch Linda shut him down. You will eat the candy Angie's rapist boyfriend brought her, and Linda didn't confiscate, although she did tell Angie off for seeing him. Karen will eat fireballs like they're jelly beans, and you will pop one in your mouth for nostalgia's sake. And then you will spit it back into the wrapper and gulp water from your mug.

Frank is on about the medicines he thinks he should be on – like I said, we all just want more drugs – and Linda will reply with quiet, but firm "I don't believe that's true"s. Next thing, Frank's accusing everyone in the place of being a damn liar, and when Linda calmly denies that, he will say that at least she is a raconteur. Linda – always in control – will ask him what that means and he will say, "It means storyteller. It's French. Aren't you glad you learned something today?"

When Linda breaks out the French, the three of you will straight cheer. She will say to Frank, "You don't speak French?"

VIII.

"You didn't tell me about your thing," Angie will say. And then she will motion to your wrist. You will look down at a line of swollen red and one lonely SteriStrip still hanging on. You will tell them that you don't know what you were trying to do. That your husband read your journal and hid everything sharp. That skin is much harder to cut through than you would have thought. Your doctor asked you if it was a cry for help. When you shrugged and said maybe, he said, "whatever that means."

Angie will tell you about her rapes. How a stranger attacked her a year ago, and her boyfriend has raped her every night since. She will tell you how they have separate bedrooms, but he comes into hers in the middle of the night. She will tell you that she already has custody of his children. Karen will tell her she needs to leave, you will back her up, and Angie will tell you how different he seemed that afternoon. Angie was here for a week before you arrived, and she won't leave before Thanksgiving. And her in-house ECT will take everything she has left.

Karen will tell you how she went like this – three swift motions down her wrist – but it wasn't really bleeding, so she went like this – three more motions, downwards this time. "Does it hurt?" you will ask her. "Oh, yeah." Yours will have stopped hurting long ago. And when she describes the migraines that put her on disability and led her to a glass of wine and a boxcutter in the backyard, you will feel small for two reasons: because you did not cut with the same strength of conviction, and because you are so jealous of her physical pain. You will shudder to think of Stella's chronic pain and chronic cheer in the face of it. You will wonder what it would be like to have pain someone could see.

You and Karen will make plans to meet up when you get out of here. And to buy bracelets. You're going to need a lot of bracelets.

IX.

Leaving will be sudden. One day you will say, "maybe tomorrow," but you always say that. Your doctor will visit late at night, after his work day at the office, and you will ask when he thinks you can leave, and all of a sudden there will be a bustle of paperwork and packing. You will get Karen's phone number and Emmaline's address. You will know that you and Angie will never cross paths again – that outside of 3 West, you are two completely different kinds of people.

Karen will say that she'll call. But she won't. And you'll wonder if she lost your number, if she wanted to call you but didn't have the strength. You will wonder if she killed herself and that will keep you from calling her, even though you've taped her number into a journal.

It will not storm while you are there. There will be no cathartic release, no electric epiphany. It will not be that easy.

Here's what you will miss: marathon weekend traffic, the convention you were supposed to take your students to, the weekend the leaves changed.

You will send a card to Emmaline for her birthday, signed by you and your husband, and anyone else you can find to help fill the space. She will send you a note with her phone number, which you will not save.

And it will take so long to earn back anyone's trust.

X.

Five months out of the hospital, you will be back to work, although not quite among the living, and you will go when your brother invites you to a comedy show. You will hear a comedian on the subject of suicide. He will say that it's a wasted opportunity. That if he were going to do it, he would rig the door to release confetti and streamers when it's opened. That he would loop *Hanging by a Moment* in the background and write _TAR under his hanging corpse. Your brother will look at you out of the corner of his eye, beginning to think up an apology. And you will laugh. Really laugh.

Bethany Proud

Beth Proud graduated from UEA with a first in Creative Writing in 2011. She has been shortlisted for the Bridport Prize, written music video treatments and short stories, and completed the first book of her online young adult series, welcometothebloodlands.blogspot.com. Her blog has attained a readership of eight thousand since its first post in January 2013. Beth is currently living in London and working on the second novel in the Bloodlands series.

Ferried Back

They have been driving for hours. The motorway, relentlessly grey, has spat them out somewhere outside Glasgow. Conversation trickled away a hundred miles ago. Now the only voices come from the radio, accompanied by the rhythmic squeak of the windscreen wipers as rain patters the windows.

The road ahead is a drizzled silver line. To their left is the Clyde, spreading like a spilt drink as they drive. To their right is hillside, rising sharply – almost vertical – with edges that are ragged with granite rubble. The road lurches sideways, flinging them against a wide-open stretch of coast. The sky is freckled with grubby gulls.

The radio begins to lose reception. Tony reaches for the dial and tries to find his way back to the play he was sort of listening to, but nothing comes. Just crackling and the occasional short burst of a word. Sighing, he turns it off.

He thinks of waking Olly and making him sit up front beside him. But Tony has used up all the usual questions earlier in the journey. How's the degree coming along? Seeing anyone at the moment? Olly had answered cheerfully enough, though he made it clear he wasn't going to tell his father any more than he had to. Yeah, he'll wake Olly. Just as soon as he can think of something to say that will warrant the awkwardness.

At the junction up ahead, there's a war memorial. A tall obelisk, its base circled by bright poppy wreaths. Just the sight of it triggers something, as if a buried snapshot has instantly unfurled in his mind. Somehow he has driven them back here, back to this corner of coast where they holidayed- what, fifteen years ago? Yes, because Olly would have been six.

At first the memory is only a single image: bleached and patchy the way photographs fade with age. But he remembers enough for it to feel important. It can't be an accident that they've driven back to this stretch of shore where they spent that one day, so completely undisturbed.

The rain begins to subside, tiny speckled scratches on the windscreen. He rolls down the window, just a fraction, and he can instantly smell the sea.

He unpicks the memory gradually. Pulls it undone, smoothes back the dog-eared corners. It's Olly who appears most clearly. Olly in red swimming shorts. He has sand in his hair, smudging his jaw, striping his shins. Olly says – no, *demands* – 'Help me climb, Dad!'

It's odd that he can't see Kate, though she must have been there sitting on the sand, or maybe paddling in the loch with her trouser legs rolled up. It bothers him that he can't see her face in the memory. Though they've been divorced for years, it's her absence now which makes him feel suddenly abandoned. It's only Olly standing there vividly, red shorts and sunburn. He's beckoning them forwards, he's beckoning them back.

He remembers helping Olly climb the mound at the beach's peaked nose, placing his child's hands on the lacework of ancient tree roots, nudging him up over rocks that were slimy with weed. He remembers the steeper rock at the top; flat like a table, its edges curved smooth by weather. He had to give Olly a leg-up. When he gave his son's back a little push, he'd pretended to complain that Olly was too heavy.

Tony isn't sure why they decided to climb. Perhaps it was to catch a glimpse of the ferry, the black belly of the boat churning at the waves. Or maybe it was just the need to feel tall in the landscape. It would have been the holiday they took when he was in-between jobs. Money was tight, but Tony hasn't forgotten the exhilaration he felt that day, standing side by side with Olly. Towering above the loch and knowing he couldn't, *wouldn't*, change a thing.

He's convinced the beach is around here somewhere. He recognises the harbour and the fishing boats nodding in the water, the squat little cottages lined up like tea caddies. The church tower poking feebly towards a vast expanse of sky. It occurs to him, catching glances in the rear-view mirror of Olly, snoozing in the backseat, that he should find the place and stop there. They could stretch their legs. They could climb the rocky mound and look out at the loch. He begins to drive with urgency; his fingertips clench the steering wheel as he picks up a gradual speed.

Tony spies the little beach up ahead. He's pleased with himself for remembering the way. Darkness is bruising the sky, the edge of night seeping into day and blurring the line between them. He turns into the car park; the tyres crunch over the gravel. He parks the car, his left arm draped over the passenger seat as he reverses. He's careful in the sparse light not to scrape the car against the rocks.

Olly stirs in the backseat and tugs the headphones from his ears. 'Dad...'

Tony jerks at the handbrake. The car is wedged beside a small patch of woodland and the trees tower above them, smothering them in a web of violet light. Tony lights a cigarette, tipping his head back and meeting Olly's fractious gaze in the mirror.

'Why've we stopped?'

'It's just for a minute. I had this idea we should stop here.' Tony tugs at the cigarette, all at once anxious and excited. 'Smoke?' He says, offering the box to Olly.

'It doesn't make you look cool, you know. Just makes you look like a twat.'

He's probably right. Tony leans his head against the cool car window. He looks out at the low-slung clouds, weeping mist that snakes it way in between the trees. It has stopped raining, but outside still has that damp look about it, as if the loch has bled through the beach and crept up to the car.

Olly yawns, flinging back his arms and extending his chest. There's something about the sleepy, throaty groan, about the sheer size of his son stretched out, that makes Tony feel small in his seat.

'Why here?' Olly says.

'Don't you remember being here?'

Olly just shrugs. Perhaps if he can show him this place they will share something. They might return to the car with a memory in common, instead of like this: two separate entities divided by age, divided because they are related.

Tony opens the door and tosses his cigarette to the ground. It sizzles on a soggy bed of amber leaves. He nods to Olly that he should follow. He begins to climb the mound, his hands clutching at tree roots and rocks to guide him as his shoes smear with the peaty, black mud. He doesn't wait for Olly but he hears hesitant footsteps behind him, the trudge of a trainer against dirt. Tony's knee buckles against the final climb and he steadies himself against a tree. The bark feels wet against his palm.

He waits there for Olly. He can almost taste the mist on his tongue; thick ash-coloured secretions folding coldness around his scalp. It makes his skin prickle.

It's just a moment: something that seems to swell from the past and leak into now. The mist clears. There's a hole through it, as if it's been torched.

Sunlight begins to throb across the loch, instantly drying the tree bark, crisping the mud. He feels warm sand scratching at his skin. He's wearing red shorts, heavy with sea water. They cling to his knees. A ferry sails across the water: it's black with a red stripe.

He turns to find Olly, but he isn't there. The dank woodland has sprouted bright grass, and heather and bracken. Tree branches that looked skinny and wiry just seconds ago have burst leafy spirals. He can't see the car any more; there isn't even a car park. The road has dissolved. It's just a dirt track with no distinct direction.

He skids on the rocks, using jagged ledges as a ladder to ferry himself down. This feels easy. His legs slide deftly. His hands are child's hand, soft and small and without any nicotine stains. The slate feels warm and silky under his touch.

His feet find ground, kicking at the sand. Tony tries to call for his son but his voice is choked by the name and his lips settle on an *oh...*

As he takes two steps forward, the sunlight drains from the sky, staining the waves translucent green like the fragments of a beer bottle. At once, he feels mist breathing at his skin again. His eyes adjust to the semi-darkness, settling over the sky's final pink cloud coiling above the blot of woodland.

'Dad?'

Tony looks back. Olly is standing on the mound behind him.

Tony says, 'Don't you remember being here at all? You, me and your mum. We came here on holiday, the summer before we moved house. You and I climbed these rocks together.'

Olly scratches a circle in the mud with the tip of his trainer. He shakes his head.

'I dunno what you're on about.' He sounds sorry, though, and not like he pities Tony. Like he wants to remember but he just can't get there. The same way Kate can't get there in Tony's memory

'We were here. All together, we were here.' Tony blinks. Night is sinking fast, and the moon is casting milky wrinkles on the waves.

'I don't remember. Dad, I'm sorry...'

Tony opens his mouth to speak. Everything he wants to say to Olly hovers from his lips, words that cling to the fog and drift away into the night.

'Just get in the car.' He can't help but feel angry: not at Olly's failure to recall that day. He's angry that they can't go back there together.

They return to the car in silence. Olly sits up front this time, giving the door a disgruntled slam. He sits there shivering in the darkness as Tony gets in beside him.

Tony places his hands on the steering wheel, but he doesn't start the engine. Not yet. He wants to be sure of what he's remembered. He wonders if Olly was even there, whether it was himself he remembered. And then, he wonders if it ever happened at all. He thinks that memories make up stories sometimes. They deceive you. He can't quite work it all out. They will have to start the car again, drive somewhere, but Tony doesn't know where they'll go now.

'I'm cold,' says Olly.

'Just a minute,' says Tony.

He isn't sure, any more. He just wants a minute to be sure.

Nick Rawlinson

Nick Rawlinson lives in Bristol. This is his second story to appear in a Bristol Short Story Prize anthology. He was the winner of the Bristol Libraries' *Bristol 1807* Short Story Competition. He has written for the theatre, academic publishers and several magazines. He has narrated several audio books by writers who include Arthur Conan Doyle, J.L. Carr, John Connolly and Ronan Bennett. He volunteers for the Unputdownable literary festival and the Friends of Henleaze Library.

ICARUS

Sparrows fall from the sky. That is the nature of things. They do not choose to fall, just as they did not choose to fly. They cannot help it. Flight is born within them. They take to the wing before the thought of space, of air. They fall before they ever dream of earth.

It is the same for everyone. Before you choose, before you even start to think, the choice has been made. Taken flight.

She knows this. She is the mother of the boy who flew. Flew and did not return. And in the numbness that followed, she looked for answers. Sat, like a human clock, marking the slow passing of days from waking to sleeping. Searching in the sigh of papers, the comfort of books. She read them all. Pictures of brain scans. Studies of synapses. Debates of the eminent philosophers, works of the greatest poets and playwrights. Made her mind scour runways of thought from which imagination and fancy and knowledge rose and fell.

No one spoke to her. No one called in. No one disturbed the concentration that wrapped itself around her, a suit of mourning. She was left alone, left to herself, to pin down arguments, to tether reason. So concentrated, even the brown hair that tumbled over her shoulder hung motionless, the tip of every strand focussed solely on the page below.

She was in a strange new world, and these were her charts, her plans of navigation. She scanned the clouds of words, ran her fingers across them, feeling for answers. And when she'd finished, she understood.

The other mothers could only watch her. And wonder. Thank Providence that they had not been blessed with such a son. Watch as she pieced it all together. Motives and feelings. Story arcs and parameters. Fact and fiction, earth and air. Watch, as she struggled to a conclusion. Do we choose, or is our story already written?

Had they asked, she would have told them. Translated the movement of the wind, the illusion of chance. Told them, there's no such thing as an accident. From the greatest step to the smallest, before you even know it, the choice has already been taken. Shall I kill the King? Split the atom? Step off the kerb? Hit the brake? Too late. It's already happened.

She knows this, and accepts it. She is the mother of the boy who flew because he had no choice. His desire for flight was manifest before he could walk, before his eyes opened, before the sun first kissed his face. It was her present to him. Her choice of his father. Creating those particular strands of aerial DNA. Or perhaps by mistake, by giving him the wrong book or the wrong toy, something that fired his childish imagination upward, puffing his chest out like a balloon until his soul only knew one direction: up. She will never understand the mechanism: only the fact. He was the boy who flew.

But if all choices have been made, why, then, does she now hesitate? Stand in the doorway of his bedroom, teetering on the very edge of going in? Her feet have brought her there, one step, another. Her fingers have tied her apron, mechanically, brain blind. In her hands are the duster, the Hoover. She has come to clean. But as yet, she does not. Nor does she know why.

It feels strange to enter his room. Like she hasn't been invited. Now, when he isn't there to make the invitation. The room is still, silent; a launch pad hush. The heartbeat of the everyday is stopped, the headlong rush of time seems suspended. Or rather falling, very slowly, like motes of dust.

His dust. The tiny fibres of his life. Clothes. Skin. He always made things a little soiled, a little dirty. Earthy. She'd never been able to keep on top of it all. His desire for flight found a counterpoint in the ground. Experiments. Models. Decals, transfers, prototypes. Drawings on the walls and smears on the furniture. He covered the carpets with paper aeroplanes and matchstick gliders. Filled the rest of the house with balsa wood and glue. You could not walk past the stairs without risking a collision. He celebrated each new birthday by jumping from a higher stair. The other mothers began to notice. Spoke of it amongst themselves. Little bird, they'd called him. Little pilot.

And as he'd grown, so had the mess. Rubber bands and feathers. Bike chains and crankshafts. New words in his mouth. Elevators. Ailerons. Lift Coefficients. And new places growing in his heart where he hid small deceptions. The money he took from her purse. The blankets he stole, and bamboo canes, making wings when he thought no one was looking.

And then. Suddenly. One day. One day when it all went quiet and she'd found him, standing, on tiptoe, on the very edge of the roof. And she remembered calling to him. And the look in his eyes. And then he just – jumped. Trailing his laughter behind him like a banner, an aviator's scarf. And in that moment, her life changing forever. And then changing back.

He'd landed, awkwardly, the ungainly fledgling. But alive. And all she could do was watch him, as he limped into the kitchen. Beyond her control, now. Dragging himself, the fallen angel. The wounded hero. His feet caked in mud, his leg wrapped in a bandage of the bush that had saved him when he fell. Nothing broken but a bit of her heart. And the flower bed.

She steps into the bedroom. Plugs in the Hoover. She twitches at the sound of the engine, the scream. But she continues. Cleans it all. Bed. Carpet. Even the sock she finds on the floor. She wants to be thorough. It was not the sock he had flown in, of course. That had been ripped when he landed. His shoe had come off, his foot had dragged. Torn holes. But she'll clean this one anyway. Just in case.

What she can't Hoover she washes. Gathers things up in big armfuls. Sheets. Curtains. Even his favourite toy. A battered old seagull. Much played with, much put upon. He'd loved it. In a boy's way. She meant, a careless way. Thrown it, so many times, across the room. She'd told him. You'll break that bird, she said. He'll rip. When his insides are on the outside, then how will you feel? But he'd not been able to resist. Sent the bird flying. Out of the window. Watching it over and over. Always feeling that pull deep within him. Like an echo. The echo of a long, long fall.

She looks at the bird, uncertain. The washing machine will give him a different kind of flight. Spinning and tumbling, tumbling and spinning, over and over.

Suddenly, she's forgotten how to breathe. It happens sometimes. Her stomach grows so tight a gasp floods the back of her throat and stops her heart. She'd cry if she could but she can't. Sorrows dart within her like startled birds. Did he tumble when he fell, she wondered? Spin, helplessly, over and over? No. She forces herself to watch, in her mind's eye, again, again, that last flight. Plays it out while her breath waits, hugged within her, until she grows calmer and her heart starts again.

He flew effortlessly, she tells herself. Her boy, with a loose-limbed grace. And so fast! The wind had barely time to ruffle his hair in passing. Only the sun had been able to keep up with him. Kiss his cheek. Lay a gentle hand on his shoulder. Hold him tenderly as he came back down to earth.

On the tiniest of details, she stumbles. In the gaps between thought and action, between neuron and synapse, in the holes between electrons, in the quantum spaces, freewill and determinism go flying, spiralling, out of control. Before the fall, the flight. Before the flight, the step. Before the step, the teetering, on tiptoes, the pause, before the scream of tyres, the flight.

She puts the bird into the washing machine and wishes she hadn't. There was a sharp nylon seam on his back; it has cut her finger. Blood blooms. She sucks it, and her tongue becomes bitter. She remembers her grandfather telling her, when you die you need a coin in your mouth, to pay the ferryman. Otherwise, he said, when they drop you into your grave, you'd better pray your soul can fly.

She remembers taking a tuppence from her mother's purse. Putting it between her lips. Wondering.

She shakes her head. Makes to leave the house. Walk out into the air. There will be stares, she knows. Everyone recognizes her, knows who she is. The woman whose son flew. Flew, but did not know how to land. One shoe off. His head kissing the road. The blood that bloomed and tumbled and spun and fell between the holes in the tarmac.

They will point her out, those other mothers, follow her with their eyes, mark her passing in the space they give her. It is as if she wears it, her sorrow: a petticoat, a bustle of grief. The air around her still and silent. Like her whole house, how it had stopped, held its breath in the moment after she was told. Her boy. He'd flown. And still she thinks of it, how the wind ruffled his hair and the sun kissed his face, as he flew, the world holding its breath.

And so much of her had died, then. Yet her feet kept walking and her heart kept beating. And she had made choices. About the service, the casket, the words to be written and said. And afterwards standing where he had stood. Wondering how it had felt when his foot left the kerb and hovered in space. Before the car. And the flight.

There's part of her that thinks if she keeps living, keeps breathing, then somewhere he'll keep flying, won't hit the ground. And she won't have to face all the yesterdays that became, so suddenly, a trail of broken flowers, left by the kerbside.

She makes a decision. Perhaps it has already been made. Takes the brand new Hoover, still full of dust, his dust, and puts it outside the garden gate. Free to a good home.

She goes back inside. Feels her heart beat.

And her tears take flight.

Judges' Profiles

Ali Reynolds (chair)

Ali previously worked as an editor at Vintage, Random House, where she commissioned collections of short stories and novels from emerging writers. She moved to Bristol to establish her own literary consultancy in 2005. A passionate advocate for the creativity and talent in Bristol, Ali is involved with the Bristol Festival of Literature and runs courses for writers. Ali has been involved with the Bristol Short Story Prize since 2010 and has been thrilled to see it evolve into the internationally recognised competition it is today. She lives with her husband and two children, who are bookworms like herself.

Bidisha

Bidisha is a writer, critic, broadcaster and human rights activist who has been writing professionally since she was 14 and signed her first book deal at 16. She writes about the arts and social issues for *The Guardian*, *The Observer*, *The Financial Times*, *The F Word* and many other publications internationally. She has been the presenter of *Night Waves* (Radio 3), *The Strand* (World Service), *Woman's Hour* and *Saturday Review* (both Radio 4) and numerous arts documentaries for the BBC. She judged the *Orange Prize* in 2009 and the *John Llewellyn Rhys Prize* in 2010. Her fourth book, the reportage *Beyond the Wall: Writing A Path Through Palestine* was published in May 2012.

Anna Britten

Anna Britten is an author and journalist. Her short stories have been broadcast by BBC Radio 4, published in the *Bridport Prize Anthology 2010*, the Bloomsbury anthology *Is This What you Want?* (via the Asham Award), *Decongested Tales*, and on US websites *Eclectica* and *Prick Of The Spindle* – and shortlisted for various other competitions including the Fish International. She has also published non-fiction and children's fiction. She is Features Editor at national monthly lifestyle magazine The Simple Things, where she also looks after the short story section. Twitter: @msabritten

Christopher Wakling

Christopher Wakling's six acclaimed novels include *What I Did* (John Murray, 2011) and *The Devil's Mask* (Faber, 2011). He is the Royal Literary Fund Writing Fellow at Bristol University, leads Creative Writing courses for the Arvon Foundation, and writes travel journalism for *The Independent*. Before he turned to writing full time, Christopher worked as a city lawyer, and before that he read English at Oxford. He lives in Bristol with his wife and children.

Acknowledgments

Without the commitment of those listed below the Bristol Short Story Prize would be much the poorer. A huge thank you for their generosity, expertise and enthusiasm to:

This year's judges – Ali Reynolds (chair), Anna Britten, Bidisha, Chris Wakling; our readers – Katherine Hanks, Lu Hersey, Tania Hershman, Richard Jones, Mike Manson, Dawn Pomroy; Chris Hill, Jonathan Ward, Emily Nash and the 3rd year Illustration students at University of the West of England; Peter Morgan and Mark Furneval at ScreenBeetle, Jane Guy and The Bristol Hotel, Peter Begen, Snoozie Claiden and Arnolfini, Joe Burt, Annette Chown, Daisy Crosby, Sara Davies, Fran Ham, Mel Harris at Waterstone's, Nicky Johns, Sylvie Kruiniger, Marc Leverton, Kathy McDermott, Natasha Melia, Rosa Melia, Rudy Millard and Guide2Bristol, Dave Oakley, Thomas Rasche and to all the writers whose stories have given us so much pleasure and inspiration.